Trouble
Times Ten

KidWitness Tales

Crazy Jacob
by Jim Ware

Dangerous Dreams
by Jim Ware

Galen and Goliath
by Lee Roddy

Ruled Out
by Randy Southern

Trouble Times Ten
by Dave Lambert

The Worst Wish
by Lissa Halls Johnson

KiDWiTNESS
T·A·L·E·S

Trouble
Times Ten

DAVE LAMBERT

BETHANYHOUSE

MINNEAPOLIS, MINNESOTA

6/2002 Benfund 5⁰⁰

A Focus on the Family book.
Published by Bethany House Publishers
A Ministry of Bethany Fellowship International
11400 Hampshire Avenue South
Bloomington, Minnesota 55438
www.bethanyhouse.com

Printed in the United States of America by
Bethany Press International, Bloomington, Minnesota 55438

Library of Congress Cataloging-in-Publication Data

Lambert, David, 1948–
    Trouble times ten / David Lambert.
       p. cm. — (KidWitness tales)
    Summary: Ten-year-old Ben has many fears as he witnesses Moses call down a series of plagues on Egypt; then, when the Israelites follow Moses out of Egypt, their escape through the parted Red Sea forces Ben to confront his greatest fear, water.
    ISBN 1–56179–883–5
    1. Moses (Biblical leader)—Juvenile fiction. [1. Moses (Biblical leader)—Fiction. 2. Fear—Fiction.] I. Title. II. Series.
PZ7.L1679Tr 2000
[Fic]—dc21   00-010803

2 3 4 5 6 7 8 9 10 11 12 13 14 15 / 07 06 05 04 03 02 01

To Faith, forever my youngest:
My Faith
My hope
My love

DAVID LAMBERT is author or coauthor of several books, including *Jumper Fables,* the 1995 winner of the Gold Medallion Award, and *Cybershock: Totally Wired.* Dave is also a contributing editor to *Guideposts for Kids* and was founding editor of *Guideposts for Teens.* He has logged in 15 years as acquistions editor for Zondervan Publishing House.

CHAPTER 1

The cool water closes over Ben's head, shocking him. He panics for a moment, holding his breath as his arms thrash frantically. Then he feels strangely calm. Surely his parents saw him fall off the dock and will rush to lift him out of the river.

He looks up; the sun is there, high above him, a bright spot filtered by the wavering water. All he has to do is move toward it. Expecting his father's face to appear there beside the sun at any moment, reaching down for him, Ben moves his arms and legs, trying to move himself upward, toward the sun, toward the air. But he has never had to swim before and doesn't know how.

Thrashing wildly now, he wants to scream but is afraid to open his mouth. His lungs feel as if they're about to burst.

Feeling mud beneath his feet, hope surges through him—he can push himself toward the sur- face now. He bends his knees and pushes himself up-

ward with all his strength. But his feet sink into the soft mud, and he floats upward only a short distance. Then his exhausted arms reach hopelessly toward the sun and he coughs out the air he has held in his lungs all this time and watches it shriek toward the surface in huge dancing bubbles. He gulps in the murky, bitter water of the Nile, and all goes slowly black around him, fading . . .

———————

And then Ben is gasping, unsure where he is. One hand gropes around him for someone, something—

And what he finds is his blanket. He touches the thing he is sitting on. He tries to stop his loud gasping. He hears his father's snoring. He is not in the Nile, or even beside it. He is on his own sleeping mat on the floor of his family's home near Rameses, in Egypt.

He hears his mother stirring. "Ben?" she asks softly. "Are you all right?"

He opens his mouth to answer, but his throat tightens and he feels tears burn his eyes. No, he doesn't want to cry after some little nightmare. Only babies cry about nightmares. Ben closes his eyes and concentrates on stifling the sobs that build in his throat. Then he feels a movement near him, and when he opens his eyes his mother is settling onto his sleeping mat beside him, a dim oil lamp held in one hand. Ben can't help it; he buries his face in her shoulder and cries.

When he is finished, he leans against her, enjoying the warmth of her hand on his back. She is plump and soft, and not much taller than he is. They sit in a small circle of lamplight. Their floor is sand, covered in most places by rugs or sleeping mats. Ben can just make out the hunched form of his father across the room. He hears, from the small room next to theirs, the sleeping sounds of his grandparents.

"Was it the river dream again?" his mother asks softly. Her sweet voice calms him, as always.

Ben nods.

She is quiet for a while, then says, "It's all right to be frightened. It was a frightening thing. But you're 10 years old now. All of that was long ago."

Yes. Ben remembers the young man who saved him. After Ben lost consciousness in the river, he awoke lying on a sandy bank. An Egyptian man, young, strong, and dripping wet, leaned over him. His expensive clothes, dark with water, were clinging to him. When Ben began to cry, the serious expression on the man's face changed to relief. "He'll be all right," he said, and then stood. Suddenly Ben's father was there, his face twisted with emotion, gathering Ben up in his arms. And Ben has not seen that man again. But he will never forget his handsome face.

Ben's mother stretches and makes herself more comfortable. "When Moses was a baby, his mother put him in the Nile in a basket to save him from Pharaoh's men, who were killing the young children of our people. The river saved his life." She smiles. "Do you think Moses would be afraid of the river?"

Ben sighs. No, Moses would not be afraid. Moses would not be afraid of anything. Every Israelite knew the story of Moses, how he had been raised in Pharaoh's own household, the adopted son of Pharaoh's daughter who had found that basket floating in the rushes along the river. Every Israelite also knew how Moses had rebelled against the treatment his people received from the Egyptians. He had fought a cruel foreman who was beating Hebrew men. In his rage, Moses had killed that Egyptian, so he had fled for his life.

"But he won't stay away forever," Ben's father and the other men all said. "He is the only one strong enough to stand up to Pharaoh. He is a hero of the Israelites, like Abraham and Jacob and Joseph. He will come back when we need him."

Yes, Moses would come back. And he would not be afraid of Pharaoh.

No, Moses would not be afraid.

But Ben was afraid of everything. Water. Rats. Bullies. The dark. Loud barking dogs. The list of things Ben was afraid of was a long list.

Why couldn't he be more like Moses?

CHAPTER 2

Early the next morning, wiping sleep from his eyes, Ben stepped from his house and blinked at the huge golden sun, still very low in the sky. It gleamed on the river a short distance from the village—one of the many channels cut by the River Nile as it wandered across its flat, fertile delta on its way to the sea.

Away from the river, in the other direction, Ben could see the gleaming city of Rameses, where Pharaoh lived. North and east of Rameses stretched the land of Goshen, where for hundreds of years Ben's people, the Israelites, had lived. But the Israelites were no longer welcome in Egypt. Now they were little better than slaves.

Ben stepped out into the narrow, sandy street and walked away from the river. His mother had asked him to run to the marketplace for some dried fish. The shortest way to the marketplace was to walk down to the river and take the river path. But

Ben would take the longer way so that he would not have to walk near the water.

He had been walking for only a few minutes when, up ahead, in a narrow passageway between two tall mud-brick buildings, he saw two dogs. They were not big dogs. But they were circling each other, growling, showing their teeth. He stood waiting, watching. Maybe the dogs would chase each other somewhere else.

He stood too long. He felt something on his shoulder, and when he looked down, there was a scarab beetle, bright and green, crawling toward his neck! With a shriek, Ben brushed it away—and heard a sudden burst of laughter from behind him. Whirling, he saw several of the neighborhood boys. One of them picked up the beetle and held it out toward Ben, a mischievous grin on his face. "Hey, you dropped your pet! Want him in your pocket?"

Ben backed quickly away.

"Come on—afraid of a little old *bug?*" one of the boys laughed. And he flung something directly at Ben, who screeched and backed away. The thing dropped near him. Just a stick.

Because Ben was small for his age and not a fighter, he relied on his words and his wits to get him out of tight situations like this. With his heart still beating rapidly and his breath quick and shallow, he opened his mouth to say something—anything—and suddenly he was drenched with cold water!

Leaping in fear, sputtering, yelling, he spun around yet again. And there was another boy from the village, still holding the dripping bucket he'd emptied over Ben's head.

"Why are you shaking, Riverboy?" the boy asked, laughing. "The water too cold? Or are you just . . . *scared?*"

Of course I'm scared, Ben thought. *And all these boys know it. Why don't they just leave me alone?*

"How about this, Riverboy? Want a bite?" And one of the boys thrust a frog into Ben's face—a dry, tired, sick-looking frog that was obviously being squeezed way too tight.

"Hey, you're hurting him!" Ben protested, and reached out and took the frog.

Frogs were one of the few things Ben wasn't afraid of. He'd had frogs for pets, in fact, and he knew that this frog needed to get back into the water if he was to survive. He held it back out to the other boy. "Take him back to the river. He's going to die if he doesn't—"

"*You* take him back, Riverboy!"

Ben hesitated. "No, I—"

"You're afraid, that's what! Just like you're afraid of bugs, and snakes, and dogs, and cats—"

"I'm not afraid of cats!"

Ben wasn't quite sure why that sent the boys into fits of laughter.

"Oh, he's *not* afraid of cats! Did you hear that? There's something he's not afraid of!"

"Maybe that's because he's never met the right cat!"

"Leave him alone," said a quiet voice.

CHAPTER 3

There was a second or two of quiet as the boys surrounding Ben turned to see who was speaking—and saw Joel, with his older brother Micah.

Joel was Ben's best friend, and bigger than Ben—big enough that these boys wouldn't be quick to tease or bully him. He was stocky, rather than slender like Ben, and already starting to show muscles on his arms and shoulders, like his father. But now, as always, Joel's face was split in a grin, and his nose was peeling—Joel's fair skin sunburned easily and constantly.

"Ha, ha, ha—you guys are real funny," Joel said. "Now if you're through with my friend here, I need him."

The other boys stood uncertainly for a moment, looking at each other. Suddenly the one who'd given Ben the frog grinned and said, "Yeah, we're done with Riverboy. After all, now we've got—Eggshell!"

The boys surrounded Micah. He looked back at them blankly.

Micah was—well, Micah was different. The boys called him Eggshell partly because of his egg-shaped head and partly because they claimed there was nothing in his head, as empty as an eggshell with the egg sucked out. Micah couldn't talk; he simply made sounds of distress or anger or misery, as a baby would. And when he wasn't making those sounds, his jaw hung open, his lips slack. He was stick-thin and small for his age, smaller even than Ben although Micah was two years older. He had Joel's unruly, straight black hair, but that was where the family resemblance ended. All you had to do was look at his deep-set, not-quite-straight eyes to see that something was wrong with Micah.

"Can you go with me to the marketplace?" Joel asked, still grinning. "I have to get some things for my mother, and you know how Micah is. If I'm looking at the vegetables, he's over pulling the candles out of the bin—"

"Sure," Ben said. "But let's be quick, because I need to leave soon or I'll be late getting to the Red House."

Ben's father and grandfather, like most of the Israelite men, worked as laborers, making bricks from mud and straw for building monuments and pyramids. But Ben, like many of the women and children, worked in the royal city of Rameses as a house servant for a wealthy Egyptian family. They lived in a huge home that Ben called the Red House because it was made from a special kind of sandstone, reddish in color, that had been brought from far away. His master, the head of the home, was a high official in the court of Pharaoh.

At the marketplace, Ben quickly found the dried fish his mother needed, but by the time Joel had found everything on his list, the sun was high.

"Better get home," Joel said, looking at the sky. "Must be about time to leave for work. You want to—"

Both boys looked up suddenly, then looked at each other. There was a commotion at the other end of the marketplace—a voice calling loudly, a crowd gathering, and the sound of feet running. Joel grabbed Micah's hand and started toward the sound, with Micah protesting loudly all the way, pulling against him.

The boys jogged up to the edges of the large group of people.

"Tell us more!" people urged.

"That's all I know," a man's voice replied from somewhere in the middle of the crowd. "Moses has returned, and he has asked to talk to the elders.

They've probably begun their council already."

A shock ran through Ben. Moses had returned?

"Now let me through, please!" the man's voice insisted. "I must spread the word to others. Please!" There was the sound of scuffling, and then of feet running away.

Moses had returned!

Ben clutched at Joel. "We must see him!"

Joel nodded excitedly, ignoring Micah's wails of impatience.

Moses!

Trembling with excitement, the boys raced after the crowd that surged through the streets, all of them chattering and tense. Suddenly Ben slowed, and Joel looked back at him.

The crowd was heading toward the river.

It wasn't just that Ben didn't *like* to walk along the river. He *couldn't*. His fear paralyzed him. His body wouldn't do what he told it to when he came near water. "I'm sorry," he said softly, looking up at Joel.

Understanding washed through Joel's eyes. "They're heading for the open square in front of the elders' hall. We'll cut behind the tanners' yard and come out on the side of the square away from the river; we can still see from there."

Ducking into a narrow alley, the boys raced past

several low mud-brick buildings and emerged at the edge of a foul-smelling open yard filled with clay vats of dark liquid in which animal hides floated. Holding their hands over their noses and mouths, they ran along the edge of the yard to another alley-way, Micah protesting all the way. They emerged at the large open-air meeting place used when the elders needed to address everyone at once. The boys found a place along the base of a pillar—far from the elders, but at least they had a good view.

"Where's Moses?" Ben asked excitedly.

Joel quickly scanned the crowd. "I don't think he's here yet."

The elders were deep in conversation with two men dressed in travel-worn, patched clothes, with traveling staffs in their hands.

Surely neither of these men was Moses! He heard an elder call one of the men Aaron. Then, to Ben's amazement, the one named Aaron gestured toward the other man and used the name Moses.

Ben and Joel glanced at each other.

Moses was so . . . *old!* His hair was mostly gray, his beard was long and scraggly. And he didn't even do his own speaking. He stood back, leaning on his staff, while the other man spoke. Moses wasn't par-ticularly big, or strong-looking—certainly not the hero-warrior Ben had always imagined. He looked more like someone's grandfather.

Micah's squawking grew louder, and Joel hurriedly reached into his market bag and drew out a handful of dried beans for Micah to play with. "What did he say?" Joel asked. "I couldn't hear."

Ben smiled. Joel might be bigger and stronger than he was, but Ben had always had sharper ears. "The other man said that God has spoken to Moses, and sent him to us to lead us out of this land to a better place—a place flowing with milk and honey."

"Flowing with *what*? What does that mean?"

"I don't know."

Micah began to loudly crunch the dried beans between his teeth.

"What are the elders saying?" Joel asked.

"If you'll hush, I can hear them," Ben said with annoyance. He listened. "They're asking how they can know that this is indeed Moses, and that all of this is true."

To Ben's surprise, some of those in the crowd began to shout out their doubts: "I remember Moses, and you're not him!" one old man shouted.

"The Egyptians will refuse to let us go—and then they'll whip us for rebelling!" another called.

As the elders and the crowd shouted their objections, Ben felt a growing sense of alarm. He saw something on Moses' face that he had not expected to see—something that frightened him. It got worse when quarrelsome men from the crowd drew nearer to Moses and Aaron. As the men from the village threatened and shouted, Ben wondered: *Was Mother wrong about Moses?*

The chief of the elders raised his hand, and the crowd grew quiet. The old man quietly asked again, "And how do we know that all of this is as you say?"

Aaron and Moses were both silent for a moment. Just as the crowd again began to grow restless, Moses raised his hand with his staff high above his head. When the crowd quieted again, Moses tossed the staff away from him onto the sandy ground.

And suddenly, where the staff had been, there was a large snake!

Ben gasped and shrank back against the pillar. The crowd, too, surged backward, away from the snake, away from Moses, shouting in surprise and fear. But Joel, clearly delighted, leaned forward. Despite his fear of snakes, Ben watched carefully. It was true—the staff was gone, and in its place was a snake, writhing, hissing!

"It's magic!" Joel whispered.

Ben shook his head. "It's a sign! God really has

sent Moses to lead us to freedom!" He jumped to his feet and started away.

"Wait!" Joel called. "He may do more tricks! Let's stay and watch!"

Ben shouted over his shoulder at Joel. "I've got to go tell my mother that Moses has returned to lead us out of Egypt!" He pushed his way through the crowd and out into the street again.

But as he ran, Ben could think of only one thing—something he had seen clearly in Moses' face. Ben had seen something there he knew well.

His mother had been wrong. Moses wasn't brave. Maybe when he was younger, but not now.

Moses was afraid.

Just like Ben.

CHAPTER 4

The next day, Ben was again late getting to the Red House. He snuck in the back way, hoping that in the hustle and bustle of preparation for the feast to be held that night, no one would notice one small boy slipping quietly down the long hallway—

A strong hand clasped him by the back of his neck. Strong fingers turned his head until he was looking back at the stern face and dark eyes of Enoch, the older Israelite boy who supervised the younger ones. Enoch's face was hard—at first. But after a moment he broke into a grin.

"You're late, Ben," the older boy said. "And there's much to do. Now hurry upstairs. You're to help her ladyship choose the linens." He gave Ben a gentle shove toward the stairway. Enoch was never resentful that Ben seemed to be a special favorite of those who lived in the Red House.

The reason Ben was late that day was that so many interesting things were happening in the village. Women, including his mother, had been huddled together in doorways or gathered in small groups in the street, whispering excitedly, their shawl-covered heads close together. Old men sat in the marketplace arguing loudly, shouting back and forth to each other.

And it was all about Moses.

But Ben was puzzled. He was hearing as much doubt and complaining from the people in the village as excitement. "He's just another homeless troublemaker from the desert, as far as I'm concerned!" one sour-faced woman had told his mother shrilly. "No good will come of it, you'll see!"

Upstairs, her ladyship sat staring at several shelves of stacked linens for table coverings, napkins, and guest towels. Ben bowed slightly as he entered the room—blushing as she looked up, smiled, and winked at him to acknowledge his tardiness. "So glad you're here, Ben," she said teasingly. "We have much—"

Her eyes rose to the hallway behind Ben, and he turned to see his lordship come up the stairs with the slow dignity he always showed. "Well, well," he said pleasantly. "Please, my dear, don't rise. And Ben, I'm glad you're here. I was hoping to speak to you. Enoch!" He shouted the older boy's name down the stairway, and Ben could hear Enoch pounding up the stairs. "Come in, come in." He motioned Ben and Enoch to stand beside his wife. "I was hoping you boys would both be here. I have something to say to you about what happened in Pharaoh's court this morning."

Ben and Enoch looked at each other with carefully guarded excitement.

"Moses, it seems, has returned." His lordship began to pace back and forth in the large room. "It's been forty years since he fled into the desert. Now he has returned and presumes to speak for your people. He asked Pharaoh . . ." His lordship paused as if thinking, looking out the window across the desert landscape. "It was ill-advised. He asked Pharaoh to let your people ignore their tasks and responsibilities for three days to go into the desert to have a festival to worship your God."

Ben looked at Enoch in confusion. Moses had asked only for three days in the desert? But last night, hadn't he said—

"Moses should have known," his lordship said, shaking his head and turning back toward them. "He has lived in this court before. Pharaoh was not pleased." He lowered his voice and took on a stern expression, imitating Pharaoh. " 'I do not know your God, and I will not let Israel go.' Then he accused Moses and his brother of enticing your people away from their work. So—" His lordship appeared apologetic. "I'm afraid that Pharaoh has taken it into his head to make things difficult for your people. He has given orders that from this day on, the laborers from among your people are to be given no straw for their bricks. They must gather their own straw. But they are nevertheless expected to make their full quota of bricks."

"But—" Ben started to protest. A quick look from her ladyship silenced him.

"And, further, I am afraid," his lordship continued, "that Pharaoh has encouraged his foremen to be, well . . . *harsh* with your laborers."

Enoch looked at Ben. Ben's father was at the brickyards, making bricks for which he was being given no straw to mix with the mud. The men would be forced to scavenge for straw, which would slow their work, which would anger the Egyptian foremen . . .

Suddenly Ben could not wait to get home. But he could not leave. A morning and afternoon of work stretched ahead of him.

———

At dusk, released at last, Ben raced home through the narrow streets of his neighborhood. The sounds he heard alarmed him: women and children weeping, angry men shouting, other men groaning in pain.

"Was Moses there to gather straw for me today?" Ben heard one man yell. "Was Moses there to take my beating from the foreman when I fell behind?"

Ben covered the final few blocks at a sprint. He dashed through the doorway of his family's home. His father and grandfather sat on small stools, their backs bare. Ben turned away, unable to look at the welts and bruises on their skin.

Ben's mother and grandmother bent over their men, damp cloths in their hands. Ben's mother looked up. "Ben, fill our bowls with fresh, cool water from the cistern, please," she said quietly.

He did, then stood against the wall in front of his father. "I heard at the Red House," he said. "I came home as quickly as I could. Is there something I can do?"

His father looked up, his eyes dull, exhausted, and hopeless. "You're a good lad, Benjamin," he said. "There is something you can do. There is no way I can gather my straw and make my bricks all in a day, and if I fail, I'll be beaten again."

"As will I," croaked Ben's exhausted grandfather, too tired even to lift his head and look at Ben.

"So, lad, we'll need you to gather our straw for

us each day, after you're done at Red House."

Ben was confused. "But, Father—it's nearly dark."

"Yes. But we'll need straw tomorrow nevertheless—enough for me and for your grandfather both."

Ben's face went cold with fear. He looked up at his mother.

"This is not a time to give in to fear, son," Ben's father said, his voice firm but not harsh, not unkind. "I have fears of my own, but still I must get up in the morning and go back to the same field where today they beat me till I could not stand. And so you too will have to ignore your fears and do what must be done." He smiled through his pain. "Tonight, perhaps it would be best if your mother went with you."

Ben shivered only a little less when he heard that he would not have to go out into the dark alone. He would still be out in the dark.

And who knew what else would go wrong, as long as Moses was stirring up trouble?

CHAPTER 5

The next morning, as Ben walked to the Red House to help clean up from the feast of the night before, he still felt both sad and angry from the sight of watching his father get ready to leave for the brick-making yards. His bruises and welts looked even worse than they had the night before, and he was stiff and sore.

Ben could not escape the voices all around him as he walked the narrow streets, voices from people standing at the corners, voices drifting out from the open doors of houses.

"Moses and Aaron were waiting to meet us as we left the brickyards yesterday!" one huge black-bearded man said. "Can you believe it? After the trouble they'd caused?"

"What did you say to them?" an elderly man asked.

"It's a wonder we didn't lay hands on them and throw them out of Egypt," the big man growled.

"The man next to me said to Moses and his brother, 'May the Lord look upon you and judge you! You have made us a stench to Pharaoh and his officials and have put a sword in their hand to kill us.'"

The other men in the group nodded their approval. "And what did Moses say?" the old man prodded.

"Ha! Moses? He said nothing. He looked frightened—as if he thought we might trounce him at any moment. We've placed our fate in the hands of the wrong man, I tell you. He's no savior. And he has no power over Pharaoh, that much is clear. We were better off before Moses came back."

———

"Come, Ben," the master of the Red House said to him that morning, smiling, as Ben helped gather the dirty bowls and cups strewn about the courtyard by the guests at the feast. "I need you for something else."

Ben followed his master into the house, where her ladyship held up some new white clothes. "For you, Ben," she said, smiling.

"Thank you," he stammered, embarrassed and happy and surprised. He touched the fine white cloth.

"Yes, I need you to look good this morning," his

lordship said. "You're coming with me to court."

Ben felt a rush of excitement. This was not the first time he'd been to court with his master. In Pharaoh's court, it was customary for important people to have their hands free, and to have servants follow them carrying everything they needed. On those trips, Ben was awed and amazed to see so many important people together in one place, talking, hurrying, getting important things done. And sometimes he even saw Pharaoh himself.

"I'm hoping to get Pharaoh's approval for plans I've been working on for months now," his master continued. "You're to carry this box." He held up an ornately carved ivory box. "It contains a small gift for our esteemed ruler. In appreciation."

A short time later, Ben followed two steps behind his master as they ascended the stairs to Pharaoh's palace. Ben wore his sparkling new white clothes and carried the ivory box.

Pharaoh's dwelling was a huge complex of buildings and courtyards and temples that stretched far in every direction. There were people scurrying everywhere, slaves cleaning, meals being served. But the most important business was always conducted in Pharaoh's court, where Ben headed, following his master. Pharaoh's throne sat massively at one end of the huge room. Groups of men stood around the edges of the room, awaiting their turn to present their cases—and their gifts—to Pharaoh.

As soon as they entered the court, his lordship stopped so abruptly that Ben almost ran into the back of him. "What's this?" he grumbled. Ben peeked around him to see. It was Moses! He was standing before Pharaoh, Aaron at his side. "It's that madman again," Ben's master said. "Well, that's sure to put Pharaoh in a bad mood. Not a good day to press for my plans. We'll wait. And I don't like waiting. Pharaoh is sure to throw Moses into prison now. The man is a murderer, after all."

Ben could not hear what was being said between Aaron and Pharaoh. But when he saw Moses lift his staff high in front of him, he knew what was coming next. Moses dropped the staff, and it immediately changed into a large snake. The crowd stirred and murmured.

"So, he's a magician too," said Ben's master. "Well, Pharaoh has magicians of his own."

And, indeed, Pharaoh turned to his own two magicians who stood always by his throne. They conferred between themselves for a short time, and then came to stand before Moses. They, too, raised their staffs—and when they dropped them, those two staffs also changed into snakes!

Ben was so disappointed he almost felt sick.

When he'd seen Moses' staff turn into a snake back in the village that first night, he'd thought nothing but God's power could cause such a miracle. But now here were heathen magicians who didn't even know the God of Abraham, Isaac, and Jacob, and they too could turn their staffs into snakes. Was his master right? Was Moses nothing but a magician?

But as Ben continued to watch, a strange thing happened. The snakes slithered slowly toward each other on the floor, tasting the cold stone with their tongues. Then they became agitated, coiling and striking at each other, fighting, throwing loops of their bodies around each other. And Moses' snake quickly won the fight. As the other snakes lay exhausted or injured, slowly writhing on the floor, Moses' snake began to swallow them headfirst, one at a time!

"Well, enough of this," his lordship said, turning and pacing from the room. "We can hire our own magician to come to the house, if we want to be entertained."

———

The next morning, Ben pulled his grandmother's cart cautiously nearer and nearer the river, close to the bluff where the yearly floodwaters carved away the soil and revealed a rich band of heavy red clay.

Staying as far away from the water as he could, he selected a part of the bluff along the river where the clay seemed dark and rich and free of pebbles and sticks.

It was this clay that his mother had sent him for. She needed it for making pottery.

Ben edged along the bluff, just a few feet from the river behind him, and began to gather handfuls of the moist, firm, heavy clay, then dropped them into the huge basket sitting in the cart.

Ben wished he were anywhere but here.

The other boys only tease me because they know I'm afraid of them, and this river—and everything else, too. And the only way to make them stop bothering me is to stop being afraid.

As he had dressed that morning, and as he had eaten, he had thought and thought of ways to overcome his fears. But the only answer he came up with, over and over again, was the one that scared him most of all: To overcome his fears, he would have to face them squarely, head on, and keep facing them until they stopped scaring him. To overcome his fear of bugs, he would have to find a bug and hold it until he was no longer afraid of it. To overcome his fear of dogs, he would have to find a dog, stand close to it, pet it, until he was no longer afraid of it. To overcome his fear of water—no, that would be too hard.

And yet there it is, Ben thought. *Right behind me. If I ever wanted to face my fear of water, this is the time. There's nobody around to tease me if I panic—and nobody around to save me, either. Just me and the river. I can stand on the bank, face my fear head-on, pick up my foot, and—*

Ben shuddered. *And what? Who am I fooling? I could never step into the water. I could never face that—*

But wait. A strange thought came to Ben. He could never face the river. But suppose he weren't facing it? Suppose he *backed* into the water?

He giggled. It was such a silly thought. And anyone who saw him would laugh himself silly.

But there was no one here to see. He was alone.

He thought again of the teasing boys.

He stopped gathering clay. He deliberately looked away from the water. Could he do it? Could he put his feet into the water if he weren't looking?

Ben gathered a few more handfuls of clay and pulled the cart away from the bluff. "Is that a frog? There, in the grass?" Ben asked himself, knowing there was no frog but needing to trick himself into coming closer to the water. "Maybe I'll take a closer look." He circled widely, walking sideways, until he was very near the river but with his back to it. "I can't see anything—maybe I need a different angle."

He took a small step backward. Then another.

Then he lifted his foot, sucked in a mouthful of air, squeezed his eyes shut—*This time I'll feel the river for sure!*—and put his foot down. "Ahh!" he yelled abruptly—and then shook his head. No water. He hadn't backed into the river yet.

But it couldn't be far. He took one more step back, hunching his shoulders and hissing through his teeth, feeling with his big toe—lower, lower— and yes, there it was! His toe was in the water!

He froze in position, unsure what was going to happen. Would he panic and run? Would a crocodile leap out of the river and devour him? He waited through one long, slow breath, then another, then a third—and nothing happened. He was still alive, he hadn't panicked. After all this time, he could do this! He wasn't over his fear, not yet, but if he had taken the first step, he knew he could take the next one.

Could he actually look at the water? He had touched it—why shouldn't he look at it too?

He would try it. He looked down from the sky toward the distant city on the horizon. Then down at the ground near his foot. Then back toward his toe that was dipped into the—

With a leap of terror, Ben hurtled away from the

river, twisting about in the air to land on both feet facing the water—

The water that had now turned to blood.

Thick, red blood.

CHAPTER 6

The Nile seems better today," Enoch whispered a few days later, as he and Ben worked shoulder to shoulder, scrubbing the tiles of the courtyard at the Red House. "Yesterday, I noticed that the blood had mostly washed on down the river, along with most of the dead fish. Today the water looks almost normal, and the birds are beginning to hunt along the shore again. By tomorrow it will be normal."

That was good news. The truth was, in the days since Moses had turned the water to blood, Ben was beginning to wish he had never heard of Moses. Everyone, Egyptians and Israelites alike, had had to find some other source of water. They had found it by digging pits near the river's edge. But that was hard work. Besides, the fish had died in the bloody river and floated by the tens of thousands in the fouled water at the edge of the river, stinking horribly. Ben had dipped several jugs of water from a pit that morning himself—standing with his back to the river. After his experience on the day the water turned to blood, Ben was more afraid of the river than ever.

"Do you think Moses will leave Pharaoh alone now?" Ben asked. "His tricks are doing no good. Life has been worse for all of us."

Enoch scrubbed the stones silently for a moment, then playfully butted Ben's shoulder with his head. "You have lost faith in him already?"

Ben thought about the welts and bruises on his father's back—even more of them since the water had turned to blood. "Maybe it's Pharaoh I don't trust. Either way, I doubt that their arguments will bring about our freedom."

More and more of the Israelites seemed to feel that way. Just that morning, as Ben had walked to the Red House, the talk on the streets of the village was all about Moses. "If he was going to curse Pharaoh and the Egyptians, why'd he curse us at the same time?" one old man had growled.

"Who asked him to help us, answer me that," his wrinkled companion had said, spitting into the sand. "We might not be rich here, but at least we didn't have trouble, not till Moses came."

"No, and all his tricks don't amount to much anyway. Pharaoh's magicians can turn their staffs to snakes, too, just like Moses, and they can turn water to blood."

That, Ben had to admit, was true. He had himself seen the court magicians turn their staffs to snakes, and he'd heard that, when Moses had turned the Nile to blood, Pharaoh had turned to his court magicians, who had likewise turned water to blood.

Enoch slopped some water over Ben's hand and chuckled when Ben drew his hand back in surprise. "Don't give up yet, Benjamin, my friend. I think Moses is doing something bigger than we understand. The day may come when we will talk to our grandchildren of these days, and they will sit spellbound as we tell of the wonders God wrought through Moses."

It was Ben's turn to chuckle. "Will our grandchildren be that interested in hearing us tell of scrubbing cobblestones?"

Enoch shrugged. "Who knows? How does anyone know, while he is trying to live through it, whether the days of his life are the stuff of great stories and tales that will be told throughout all time?"

The boys worked quietly, thinking about what Enoch had said, until Enoch sat back on his haunches and laughed. "And how about you, little one?" He reached to the side and picked up a small green frog. "Do you think we are living in days that will become legend? And where did you come from, anyway?"

Ben pointed with his scrub brush toward the courtyard wall. "He came with his friends." Two more frogs sat in the shade of a potted palm, one of them squatting on the foot of the statue of the frog-god, Haket, in its little garden shrine.

"So he did," Enoch said. "It is odd, though. I have not seen frogs in the—"

Suddenly there was a shriek from somewhere across the courtyard, and Ben and Enoch both jumped to their feet. Enoch tossed the frog into his bucket of water as they raced toward the sound.

The shriek sounded again, and now the boys could tell that it was coming from the kitchen. Enoch made it to the doorway first, and Ben, right at his heels, burst into the kitchen and saw that Naomi, the Hebrew cook, was standing on a stool, her flour-covered hands over her mouth. She pointed toward her worktable. "Get them! Quickly! Please! I have no idea how they got in there!"

Enoch and Ben rushed to the worktable and peered into a huge bowl full of batter.

A half dozen small grayish tree frogs slogged through the heavy batter or stumbled across its surface, their feet and legs so coated that they could barely move.

"Quickly! Get them out of here!" Naomi insisted shrilly.

But Enoch just glanced up at her, then looked at Ben, one eyebrow raised. "Well, I'd heard Moses had something else up his sleeve. I think we just discovered what it is."

CHAPTER 7

J oel, Ben, and Micah stood in the street in front of Joel's house, looking for frogs. They had agreed the night before to get up early and search for the biggest frogs they could find to keep as pets. And there should have been plenty of them. The day before, by the time Enoch and Ben had helped Naomi get the frogs out of her batter, frogs had been everywhere. They were coming out of every hole in the ground and the walls, and were swimming in every liquid. Frogs were climbing in every potted plant the mistress had placed around her home.

And this morning, the three boys were surrounded by frogs—all dead. Every frog on the street, and there were thousands if not millions of them, was dead. Tree frogs, toads, big green frogs, smaller brown frogs with yellowish legs—they all lay still, looking shrunken and dry.

"What happened to them?" Joel asked.

Ben shook his head. "I don't know. Do you

suppose Pharaoh agreed to Moses' demands, and so Moses caused the frogs to die?"

Joel snorted, kicking at a pile of dead frogs. "Or else Pharaoh's magicians killed them. Didn't you hear that, after Moses and Aaron caused the frogs to come out of the river, Pharaoh asked his magicians to make frogs come forth, too—and they did? So far, every trick Moses has pulled, Pharaoh's court magicians have done the same thing!" Joel shook his head. "Why should we think Pharaoh will listen to him?"

Ben poked a stick among the dead frogs, hoping to find one still moving that he could revive with a little water. "All I hear is people saying they wish Moses would just go away so things could get back to normal." He waved his hand in front of his face, trying to clear away the cloud of gnats that arose from the frogs when he disturbed them.

"You boys!" someone yelled, and Ben and Joel looked up. One of the elders strode down the lane, holding part of his loose sleeve in front of his face. "Find something to use as a rake and begin pulling all of these dead frogs into big piles so they can be hauled away. They're starting to stink and to attract gnats. Quickly! Everyone must help!"

Ben and Joel looked at each other and shrugged. They weren't going to find any live frogs for pets anyway. And they couldn't disobey an elder.

————————

By the time the frogs were raked up, the gnats had become worse than the stink of the rotting frogs—and it was obvious to everyone that the presence of the gnats wasn't natural: Moses had done it again.

Ben tossed aside the forked stick he'd been using as a rake and ran back home; it was time to gobble some food and hurry off to the Red House. His mother had a scarf tied across her face when he rushed into their house. "Oh, Ben," she moaned. "These gnats! I'd rather have the frogs! At least you can pick up a frog and throw it away—but what can you do about these gnats?" She brushed several of them away from her face, then handed Ben a bowl of porridge. "This isn't much, I know—I'm sorry. But with these gnats—"

Ben grabbed a piece of bread to dip into the porridge, then stopped. "There are gnats in it!" he cried.

"Well, scoop them out," his mother said wearily, sitting near him and pulling her head cloth closer around her face so that nothing but her eyes showed. "I'm sorry, but what can I do? They're everywhere."

Ben took a bite of his bread—and immediate spit

it out. "*Pfah!* There are gnats in my mouth!" He looked at the piece of bread in his hand. Gnats swarmed all over it. He looked up at his mother to yell out his frustration, but as he opened his mouth to suck in a breath, he got more gnats than air and immediately choked. He tried swiping the gnats out of his mouth with his fingers, tried spitting them onto the ground, but in the end he swallowed most of them. Tears sprang into his eyes.

His mother pulled him close to her. "I don't understand this," she said. "Since Moses came, we've had nothing but more work, bruises, and mouthfuls of gnats. I just don't understand."

––––––––

But that evening, as Ben and his family struggled to eat dinner without eating more gnats than food, they were all strangely excited, despite the annoyance. "The master was very upset this afternoon," Ben said gleefully, pulling aside the scarf that covered his mouth and nose. "This time, Pharaoh's magicians *couldn't* make the gnats appear from the dust, as Moses did! And they even admitted to Pharaoh that they thought it was the hand of God that caused the gnats to appear, and that he'd better listen to Moses!"

Ben's father nodded, hungrily shoving into his

mouth a piece of bread dipped in the meat-and-vegetables dish Ben's mother had prepared. There were gnats all over it, but his father didn't seem to care. "And while our Egyptian overseers seemed as cruel and impatient as ever," he mumbled around the mouthful of food, "they also seemed worried."

Ben's mother shook her head, still swathed in cloths to keep the gnats away. "We're fooling ourselves. Pharaoh won't listen. And besides, we're as bad off as the Egyptians—we have to suffer through the gnats, too! If Pharaoh doesn't listen this time—which he won't—then what will Moses unleash on us next? If Moses is supposed to be our savior, then he's saving us to death!"

Ben was at the Red House two days later when he discovered just what it was Moses—and God—would unleash next.

Ben hadn't noticed much out of the ordinary at first—just a few more flies than usual—until the master rushed home early. "Enoch!" he yelled, sweeping into the house's main salon on the first floor and tearing off his cloak. "Gather everyone! I want every window covered, every door, every opening in the house! Pharaoh's court is already overrun, and they're moving this way!"

"What, sir?" Enoch asked, bursting breathlessly in from the courtyard.

"Flies," the master said impatiently, pointing at a few that were crawling along the wall near the window. "Don't just stand there! We'll soon be drowning in them if you don't move! Get everyone, the entire household! Find every sheet, every towel, and cover everything! Keep them out! *Move!*"

Everyone in Egypt knew that flies were more than just an annoyance; they often carried disease. Enoch barked out his orders, and Ben and the other servants in the household leaped into action. Soon, while the master and mistress and their children huddled in an inner room, Ben and the others were racing through the house with armloads of cloths pulled from every chest and cabinet in the house, trying their best to cover every opening to the outside, but it wasn't working. The flies were growing more numerous every minute.

Suddenly Ben heard his master's voice bellowing from the room where he and his family had taken refuge. "Ben!"

He rushed into the room. The entire family huddled on the floor in the middle of the room under an immense cotton cloth.

"Is no one taking care of the animals?" the master barked.

"No one, sir. You told us all to—"

"Take two others and go out to the pens. Bring all of the animals into the barn."

"Yes, sir," Ben said and ran from the room.

Outside, the sheep and goats were running back and forth across their pens trying to escape from the flies. "Azariah!" Ben yelled to the smaller of the two boys he'd brought with him. "Go into the barn and close all the doors and windows! We'll bring the animals to you!"

When the last sheep had been shoved into the barn, Ben said to the other boy, "Come on, Nathan—now the ducks and the geese."

"What about them?" Nathan asked, sobbing, the tears striping his dirty cheeks. "Just leave the ducks and geese."

"We can't just leave them," Ben said, regardless of how badly he wanted to do just that. "The master said—"

"I don't care!" Nathan shouted, slapping violently at the back of his neck, at his shoulders, at his arms. "They're biting me *through* my clothes!" And he turned and ran—not toward the Red House, but toward home.

Ben wanted desperately to follow him, but he was afraid of what his master would do to him if he disobeyed. "Azariah!" Ben yelled as he tried to brush away the flies crawling up his legs. "Are you all right?"

"I guess so," the younger boy answered, his voice shaking. "They're not quite as bad in here."

"I've got to go do something about the fowl," Ben said. He ran around the barn and pushed through the gate into a wide pen dominated by a shallow pond. The ducks and geese inside were panicked, rushing from side to side, their wings spread and flapping, running into the woven fence of the enclosure trying to escape from the flies.

Honk!

The sound was so sudden, so loud, and so hostile that Ben looked up in surprise, forgetting about the flies. There were three huge ganders, their eyes blood-red and angry, their immense wings spread, their necks outstretched—and they were coming for *him!*

Ben turned and ran. He made it through the gate, but not before one of the geese had bitten him painfully on the calf. And as he dragged his leg through the opening, that gander came through the opening too before he could slam the gate shut behind him. The huge goose lunged forward, its beak snapping, grabbing his clothes, trying to get to his face—

Ben turned and ran for home, yelling, slapping

at his body and at the air around him, fleeing from the goose that still snapped at his heels, swatting at the flies that bit and swarmed and crawled under his clothes and into his eyes . . .

Until suddenly the flies weren't crawling across his face anymore. Ben stopped in surprise, then quickly turned and looked behind him. No, the goose was gone, too. Ben had been running for some time; he was already back to the edge of the Israelite village. He shook himself like a dog shedding water, getting the last of the flies off, and then looked around in wonder. A few flies here and there, but nothing unusual. A normal day.

Then he looked back toward the city of Rameses. It was too far away for him to see the flies themselves, but he could see a cloudy effect in the air caused by the swarms of flies, and he could see people and animals running, slapping at something. Yes, the flies were still there.

But not here.

And then he remembered what his mother had said the night before: *We're as bad off as the Egyptians—we have to suffer through the gnats, too!* Had Moses finally done something right—hurting Pharaoh and the Egyptians in a way that didn't also hurt the Israelites even more?

The breeze from the river brushed through Ben's hair, and he lifted his face to enjoy the lightly scented air, so free of flies or gnats.

CHAPTER 8

Two days later, Ben spent a hard afternoon in the hot sun, a cloth tied across his face to fight the smell, helping the servants from the households in Rameses drag the carcasses of goats, sheep, and other livestock to the edge of town, where they were piled and burned.

Hundreds of animal carcasses.

Thousands.

Ben had been amazed when Joel had awakened him that morning, hissing from the doorway, with the news—all of the animals owned by the Egyptians had died during the night. But all of the animals of the Israelites were still alive.

Actually, not *all* of the Egyptian animals had died. Moses had warned the Egyptians, the day before, that if they would take their animals out of the fields, and put them in their barns, the animals would be spared. But Pharaoh had scoffed at Moses' words, and left his animals in the fields, and so of course the rest of the people of Rameses had done the same.

And only those few animals in the barns had survived whatever sudden sickness had killed the rest.

Even so, Pharaoh had not agreed to let the Israelites go into the desert to make their sacrifices and worship God.

———————

As Ben walked through the streets of Rameses the next day on his way to the Red House, he was surprised to see no Egyptians on the streets, only Hebrew servants, rushing on urgent errands. When he got to the Red House, he found out why: His lordship and her ladyship and all of their children lay moaning and complaining in their soft beds, their skin bare because of painful boils that covered them everywhere. The Israelite servants, none of whom were afflicted with boils, scurried back and forth between the bedrooms and the kitchen, hauling bowls of cool water into which Naomi had poured a little vinegar. Ben and Enoch and the others sponged the red, swollen skin of the Egyptian family with the vinegar-water to try to bring some relief to them in the hot desert air.

Later, on their way to the kitchen for fresh water, Ben and Enoch stopped in the courtyard in the shade of a palm tree for a moment. "Have you heard of any of our people with boils at all?" Enoch asked.

Ben shook his head. "None. How did this happen?"

"Haven't you heard?" Enoch asked. "It's another of Moses' plagues. He and Aaron brought handfuls of soot to Pharaoh's court this morning and flung it into the air. The wind carried it high over the city and farther, over the whole land of Egypt. Then it rained down, and all of the Egyptians were suddenly stricken with painful boils. I heard that Pharaoh asked his magicians to copy Moses' feat—or, better yet, make it go away." Enoch chuckled. "But they were in such pain from the boils that covered their bodies that they could do nothing."

Ben thought. "None of our livestock died yesterday, and none of our people have boils today. And the flies left us alone, too. God has decided to spare us from the plagues He is visiting on the Egyptians."

Enoch nodded, then grinned. "I guess Moses is doing something right, after all. Remember how little faith you had in him, my friend?"

Ben snorted. "Pharaoh hasn't let us go yet. Either he ignores Moses and the plagues, or else he agrees to let us go and then changes his mind as soon as God removes the plague. And I don't hear many people in my village who want to go, anyway. They're afraid to go."

Enoch raised an eyebrow, and Ben blushed. Enoch knew, as did everyone else, of Ben's fears. But Enoch never teased him. "If it is God's will for us to leave Egypt," Enoch said, "then we should be afraid to stay."

———

By the third day, most Egyptians had recovered enough to tend to their business, although their skin was still tender.

Once again, the sound of sheep, goats, and cattle echoed from the pens in back. On the same day the plague had killed the Egyptians' animals, Ben's master had, like most of the other wealthy Egyptians, sent servants out to neighboring lands to buy more livestock and bring them back, and the first of them had begun to arrive the day before.

As he gathered up the linens that had been hung out to air that afternoon, Ben noticed Enoch talking quietly with another Israelite who served in the palace, running errands. After the other servant had scurried away, Ben motioned Enoch over and asked, "Is there news?"

Enoch nodded. "Moses has promised a hailstorm, the worst storm ever to afflict Egypt. He has given Pharaoh and the Egyptians a day to bring their new livestock into the barns for protection. The storm will come tomorrow morning."

Ben was surprised. Hail? He had heard of this ice that falls from the sky, but had never seen it. Even rain was not common in this part of Egypt; their water came from the river. "We'll see hail!" he said excitedly.

Enoch shook his head. "It's not likely to be fun— the whole purpose is to make Pharaoh and the Egyptians suffer because they won't listen to God. I wouldn't want to be caught out in it."

Ben nodded slowly. Yes, but . . . hail! He'd never seen it. And tomorrow he would.

The next morning, Ben and Joel and Micah went out into the fields to gather straw. The Egyptian taskmasters still expected the Hebrew men to provide their own straw for making bricks. And straw was becoming harder to find.

But today, Ben didn't mind. And Joel felt the same. Out in the field is exactly where they wanted to be. "When is the hailstorm supposed to start?" Joel asked.

Ben shrugged. "This morning sometime. Look at those clouds." He pointed toward the dark, looming clouds piled high to the west.

Joel nodded. "It might be soon. And where do you suppose it will fall?"

"Where? What do you mean?"

"I mean the flies were bad throughout Egypt, or so we've heard—*except* where we Israelites live. The boils didn't affect us, our livestock didn't die when—"

"Ah," Ben said. "I see. So when the hail falls . . ."

"It will miss us, and hit the Egyptians," said Joel. "So if we want to see the hail . . ."

Ben nodded. "You know—I think we might be able to gather more straw in the fields over toward the city of Rameses today. We haven't gathered there yet."

"Just what I was thinking," said Joel. He shouldered his bags for straw-gathering, and Ben tugged his grandmother's cart behind him. Joel touched Micah's arm and motioned for him to follow.

They felt the first drops of rain before they had covered half the distance between their village and Rameses, and looked up in surprise. The clouds that had been looming in the west were now overhead and moving rapidly. The rain increased, and the boys stopped to watch in wonder as the clouds sped across the sky, soon covering the sun. A cold wind blew across them, making their now-damp skin shiver. Micah gave a low, uneasy moan.

And then they saw their first hailstone.

It landed with a pebbly rattle in the wooden bed of Ben's cart. The boys didn't realize at first what had made the sound, and they gathered around the cart. There it was—a tiny ball of white, about the size of a pea. Joel picked it up, and a delighted smile spread over his face. "It's cold!" he said in awe. "*Very* cold!"

Ben held out his hand, and Joel dropped it into his palm. Ben pinched it between his thumb and forefinger. He had lived his entire life in the desert, so this tiny ball was the coldest thing he had ever felt.

And then one hit him on the head. He was surprised at how much it stung. When it bounced to the ground in front of him he realized it was about twice the size of the one he'd held. Then another hit, and another, and soon hailstones were falling everywhere. They stung, and they were cold, and the boys were getting thoroughly wet, but Ben and Joel grabbed each other's hands and danced and twirled and wrestled and ran, laughing with the sheer joy of this new thing they'd discovered.

But the size of the hailstones grew. From the size of beans they grew to be the size of almonds, then grapes.

"Ouch!" Joel said uneasily. "This hurts!"

Micah moaned again and crowded close to the boys.

Then one the size of an apricot hit Ben on the head, and it hit so hard Ben felt with his hand to make sure he wasn't bleeding. "Come on!" he said. "Let's get under something!"

"What?" Joel said, looking all around. "Hey—those palm trees!"

A small group of palms grew a short distance away, and Ben grabbed one side of the now-wailing Micah, Joel grabbed the other, and they raced to the trees. They huddled in the middle of the small grove, but the hailstones—now the size of Ben's fist—shredded the fronds of the palms and fell on the boys almost as intensely as when they'd been in the open.

"This is no good!" Joel said in a panicky voice, trying to tuck the frantic Micah under his body. "Come on—let's hide in that old furnace!"

Ben turned to look. It was a brick-making furnace, huge and abandoned. "Come on, then!" he yelled, and they rushed through the pounding hail, slipping and falling on the muddy ground. They dove, bruised and filthy, into the sooty, dark furnace.

Then they were safe. The furnace was covered except for a round chimney-hole in the middle. The walls of the furnace were thick, made of heavy bricks, and although the hail made a horrible racket pounding on it, the boys knew that the furnace would stand.

A fist-sized hailstone rolled into the furnace, becoming covered with a layer of black soot. Micah picked it up and immediately began sucking on it. Joel knocked it from his hands. "Dirty, Micah! Leave it alone!"

Micah yelled in anger, then stepped outside into the storm, trying to catch another hailstone to suck. But he looked up, and a large one exploded on his face, and he screamed. Ben and Joel wrestled him back inside, and Joel reached out to find a big clean one for Micah to hold against his sore cheekbone. "Good thing it didn't hit his eye, or his nose," Joel grumbled.

Then they stood quietly, just inside the furnace, looking out across a dark, obscured world rapidly being turned into a wasteland.

"Ben," Joel said quietly. "Stop it. You're scaring Micah."

Ben turned and looked. Micah was looking at him with big, scared eyes and was beginning to moan in the way he did when frightened.

"Look normal," Joel whispered. "Your face is white, you're trembling . . ."

Ben took a deep breath, closed his eyes, and looked away from Micah, willing his legs and hands to stop trembling. And he was as thoroughly frightened and miserable as he ever remembered being in his life.

"Come, Ben," his master said early one afternoon several days after the hailstorm, hurriedly pulling on his headdress. "I've just been summoned to Pharaoh's court. Moses has arrived and demanded—demanded, mind you—to speak to Pharaoh. I want you to come."

"Yes, your lordship. Is there something you wish me to bear for you?"

"Not this time, Ben," he said as they rushed out into the street. It had been growing warmer day by day, and would soon be summer. "I simply want you to hear what Moses says, so that you can report it back to your parents, to the others in your village. I doubt that your people understand how unreasonable Moses is, and how he threatens all Egypt with these plagues."

Ben didn't know about that, but he did know that there had been many rumors in his village lately: Moses and Aaron had been killed; Moses and

Aaron had fled Egypt; Pharaoh had finally agreed to let the Israelites leave Egypt; yes, Pharaoh had agreed, but then he had changed his mind and demanded that all Israelite men be jailed and beaten; Moses had announced a new plague—lions would prowl the streets of cities throughout Egypt. No one seemed to know what Moses was up to. Perhaps Ben could find out.

But even though they hurried, sweating in the hot sun, Ben and his master arrived too late. Moses and Aaron, looking stern and angry, were stalking out of the court. And right behind them came some of the court officials and even a few of Pharaoh's soldiers, looking equally angry, muttering among themselves and pointing at the two departing Hebrew men.

"What is it, Horus?" asked Ben's master of one of the officials.

The man spat on the ground. "Called down another plague. Moses said that locusts such as we had never seen before would cover all the land and devour everything the hail didn't destroy. Then they turned on their heels and walked out. Pharaoh never said a word. His advisors and magicians are with him right now, trying to convince him that he has to respond somehow—Moses has already shown that his God can bring a powerful plague. If these locusts are as bad as he said they'd be . . ."

But Ben's master just shook his head. "No," he said quietly, almost as if he were talking to himself. "Pharaoh will not listen to reason. And he will not grant Moses' request. He will never let the Israelites go."

———————

The locusts came the next day. Soon after he awoke, before his father and grandfather had even left for the brick-making yards, Ben heard the muffled, anxious voices of people out in the streets. His mother and father looked at each other, but no one spoke; they all knew what Moses had foretold. Ben slipped out the door and joined the crowd gathering there.

A warm wind from the east ruffled Ben's hair— the same wind that had been blowing since the day before, and that he had heard rustling things outside all night long. People were gathered in groups everywhere, talking quietly, pointing at the sky. A few locusts crawled on the ground already, but most were high overhead; clouds of them were coming from the east, riding that wind and creating a dark smudge across the whole sky.

By mid-morning, the clouds of locusts were so thick the sky was darkened. And on the ground, they were everywhere—just as the frogs, the gnats, and the flies had been. But when they landed, they didn't just sit. They ate. Everything. Every green plant. Cloth, wood, leather, bread—anything their sharp little mouths could chew. They left behind only dirt, brick, stone, and bone.

Instead of cowering inside, as he would have before, Ben walked away from the village, past the houses and out into the fields. *This is one more chance,* he thought, *to show myself—and everyone else, too—that I'm not as frightened of things as they think.* He stopped brushing the locusts off his clothes—although he still brushed them from his face. He closed his eyes and stepped across the ruined field, feeling the crunch of locusts beneath his sandals. He could feel them crawling over his clothes, over his skin, across his hair, and wanted to scream, wanted to brush them off, but he forced himself to ignore them, to let them crawl.

Little scratchy feet across his hands.

The whir of locust wings next to his ears.

Run! his fear screamed. *Shake them off, brush them off, stomp them off, and then run home where it's safe!*

But he didn't shake, didn't brush, didn't stomp, and he knew that home wouldn't be any safer anyway. He had watched his mother that morning, near panic as she and Ben's father tried keep the locusts out, or at least kill all those that managed to get in.

Ben stopped walking. Slowly, he opened his eyes. He looked down at his arms, his hands, his legs. Locusts everywhere—brown grasshoppers crawling all over him, chewing at his clothes. He fought the fear, the panic, that screamed at him to run. He simply stood, trembling.

And when he looked up, there was Joel, covered with locusts.

Joel laughed. "Ben," he said, "I'm proud of you. Look at you! They're all over you—and you're not afraid!"

Ben managed an uneasy smile. "Well—I am afraid, really."

"Even better! I mean, I'm not afraid of locusts, so when I stand here like this, it doesn't mean I'm brave. But you're afraid of them—when you stand here like this, that takes courage."

Ben was surprised. Yes. He'd never thought of it that way. It wasn't really that the other boys were braver than he was. They simply weren't afraid of the things he was. There was a difference.

"I just thought of something, Joel," Ben said.

Joel raised one eyebrow, his way of asking what Ben meant.

"Just think what kind of power it took for God

to make all these things happen. All these locusts. The hailstorm. Turning the river to blood, and all the rest. A God who can do all those things can do anything. Anything!"

Joel nodded. "I suppose. But Pharaoh—"

Ben shook his head. "Pharaoh will lose, Joel."

Joel looked surprised. "You mean Moses will win?"

"Not Moses." Ben brushed away a locust that landed on his chin. "God. The Master of All. We've been thinking all along this was some kind of contest between Pharaoh and Moses. But all Moses is doing is saying what God tells him to say. Pharaoh doesn't know it, but he's fighting against God. And Pharaoh can't beat God! He just hasn't realized it yet."

f God has already won," Ben said in a low voice, "if He really is more powerful than Pharaoh, then why are we still here?"

He and Enoch walked side by side through the streets of Rameses, leaning toward each other, Ben's shoulder rubbing Enoch's elbow, so that they could speak quietly and still be heard. It was early afternoon, several days after the locusts had all been blown away on a strong wind from the sea. And yet Pharaoh, to no one's surprise, had once again refused to let the Israelites leave.

"Why is God waiting for Pharaoh to change his mind and say we can go?" Ben continued.

"Shhh," Enoch cautioned him, glancing around. "Everyone is upset. Just trust God and wait."

Ben almost laughed. "I do trust God, Enoch. But what is He—"

A fist-sized rock crashed off the building next to Ben and bounced into the street, leaving a white mark on the wall. Ben and Enoch both jumped, then glanced all around. And everywhere they looked, they saw hostile faces, any one of whom could have thrown the stone. "Go away, Hebrews, and leave us in peace!" someone shouted. "Tell your Moses that your problems are not our fault!"

"Come, Ben," Enoch whispered. "Hurry."

Only when they were safe in the courtyard of the Red House did Enoch pull Ben behind a palm tree and say quietly, "It isn't just that God is more powerful than Pharaoh. Of course He is. But He has also proven Himself to be more powerful than the gods of the Egyptians."

Ben was confused. "There are no other gods. There is only one God, the God of Abraham, Isaac—"

Enoch waved his hands impatiently. "I know that, Ben. Of course there is only one God. But don't you see? God is using these plagues to prove that to the Egyptians. What gods do the Egyptians worship?"

Ben shrugged. "They have so many gods I can't keep them all straight. There is Hapi, the god of the Nile—"

Enoch grinned. "Yes, and what did God do to his water?"

Ben's eyes opened a little wider. "Turned it to blood."

"Could Hapi stop God from doing that?"

Ben shook his head.

"What other gods?"

Ben pointed toward the squatty statue in the bubbling fountain in the corner of the courtyard. "Haket. The frog god."

Enoch nodded, still grinning. "You see? What did the Master of All do with Haket's frogs? Neither Pharaoh nor his gods are a match for our God."

Ben nodded. "Yes—I said this same thing to Joel on the day the locusts came. And soon, Pharaoh and the Egyptians, too, will know who is Master of All."

The boys sat quietly, thinking, watching a flock of geese fly high above. "What will God do next, then?" Ben asked. "Which Egyptian god will He embarrass next? And when? The Egyptians already hate us because of the plagues. Their crops and their livestock are gone. Even our own people are getting more and more angry and upset. My father and grandfather are being beaten worse than ever at the brickyards. If things get any worse—"

"They will get worse," Enoch said. "They have to, if God is to prove Himself to the Egyptians." Then he shrugged. "I don't know what will happen next. But I believe this: Before we leave Egypt, God must show that He is more powerful than the highest Egyptian god of all."

Ben looked up into Enoch's earnest eyes and nodded. "Ra," he said. "The god of the sun."

No one was surprised, an hour later, when the wind from the southwest picked up. This was, after all, the time of year for the *khamsin,* the hot desert wind. And no one was surprised to see the sunlight begin to dim as vague clouds of reddish-brown sand and dust began to move across the sky from the southwest; the *khamsin* often carried such clouds of dust. But when, by mid-afternoon, the sky was as dark as twilight, and the mistress ordered all the lamps lit in the house, people began casting worried looks outside and muttering to each other in low, serious voices. Never before had the sand carried by the *khamsin* made the sky so dark in the middle of the day.

The mistress walked into the storeroom where Ben was sorting and counting candles. "Have we enough?" she asked quietly.

"Yes," Ben said. "More than enough. Enough to last for many days."

She nodded, then counted the jars of oil. "But I would like to have ten more jars of oil this size. Run over to the merchant's shop and tell him to bring ten more before nightfall."

"But we always have these dust storms this time of year, your ladyship."

She was so distracted she didn't even reprove him for arguing with her. "I fear that this one is different, Ben. I sense the hand of Moses in this darkness. And I expect the worst."

By the time Ben had placed the order for the oil and started back for the Red House, it was almost as black as night. And the air was thick with sand, so thick and dark that he couldn't see more than a few feet ahead. He walked with one hand trailing along the stone wall to his left so that he would know where he was, and one hand holding a fold of the light cloak he wore across his nose and mouth, his eyes squeezed into slits.

Now and then, huddled shapes would pass near him, their feet shuffling along the gritty cobblestones of the sidewalk, their arms outstretched to keep them from bumping into something they could not see. Few people were out. No one spoke.

The wall to his left ended. To get back to the Red House, he would have to cross the street here. He turned and set his back directly against the corner of the wall so that he was heading—he hoped—straight across the street. He took a deep, gritty, choking breath and set out into the rapidly darkening murk. Now he could only see as far as his outstretched hand, and the wind drove the grains of sand against his skin with such force that they stung.

One step at a time, one foot in front of the other, short steps. How far had he come—maybe halfway across the street? There was no way to judge. But if he kept on as he was—

Ben cried out in a sudden rush of fear as something bumped hard and fast against his legs, and he spun, crashing to the ground with a thud. The air rushed out of his lungs, and he lay still, moaning, trying to catch his breath. What had it been? A dog? A goat?

He felt around him. He had no idea which direction he should move.

The darkness was complete now. He could see nothing, not even his hand in front of his face. Ben was so terrified by the darkness that he almost found it impossible to move. And then he realized why. This darkness, so thick with sand and dust, was closing over him just as the Nile had closed over his head when he'd fallen in years before. Cutting off all light, making it impossible to breathe, choking him . . .

He fought the fear. He had to move.

On his hands and knees, his cloak pulled over

his head, Ben crawled for what seemed like hours, bumping into walls and then following them, with no idea which way he was heading. *God,* he prayed, *God of Abraham, Isaac, and Jacob, please hear my prayer. I know that You are sending this darkness to show Pharaoh and the Egyptians that You are the only God—but I am only an Israelite, caught in the middle of Your lesson. I want to go home!*

Tears dripped from his closed eyes. His hands and knees were raw and sore from crawling. But he kept going. Soon he realized that the ground over which he crawled was now rough and uneven, and softer—he was no longer on the street, but on open, unpaved ground. Where was he? He tried to think of somewhere in the city that wasn't paved.

Then he began to climb a soft hill of sand—a dune. There were no sand dunes in the city. He had somehow crawled right out of the city.

After he had crawled over several dunes, scraping through scrubby desert bushes sometimes, he realized that the wind wasn't quite as loud. Then he noticed that there was actually a little light filtering through the cloak over his head. He pulled it aside a little and peered out. Yes—the storm was letting up just a little.

At the top of the next dune, Ben stood carefully, bracing himself against the wind that remained, and cautiously looked out through his slitted eyes.

He knew where he was. He stood on the dunes that sat southwest of the village where he lived. He thought he could just make out his village in the valley below him. He began to walk down the dunes.

Something rustled in some scrubby bushes near him, then broke free and began running rapidly toward him. With a cry, Ben turned to run, tripped over a trailing end of his cloak, and fell face-first into the sand. He looked up in time to see a rabbit scurrying away.

A rabbit. Just a rabbit, and Ben's heart was beating as if he were about to die. Is there nothing he wasn't afraid of?

He had only been fooling himself when he had felt so triumphant about overcoming his fear of the locusts. So what? There would always be something else to frighten him. He would never be a man, strong and unafraid, like his father. A man? Ha! He would never even make a good boy, like Joel, who could do the things he wanted without having to worry first about his fears. Ben was more like a girl.

CHAPTER 11

Ben sat in the small, sandy space behind his family's home, stroking the lamb tied there on a leather leash. He was waiting for Joel, but he was in no hurry. He liked the lamb. It pushed its head against his hand, enjoying the attention, bleating softly now and then. Ben wanted to name the lamb, to make it into a pet, but there was no point. The lamb would be dead in a week, killed by Ben's grandfather.

"I'm sorry; little one," Ben said, nuzzling the lamb's soft wool. "You don't know what's coming." Then he chuckled. "None of us know what's coming, do we? We've surely learned that in these past months."

Pharaoh had, once again, refused to let the Israelites leave Egypt. The storm of darkness had terrified Ben, but it had not convinced Pharaoh.

"I'm sorry; I know that Moses is supposed to be one of us," Ben's grandfather said inside the house, and Ben could hear his feet in the sand as he paced back and forth across the room. "But he's never even lived among us! Raised in Pharaoh's palace! Then for forty years he lived in the desert—and even took a wife from the desert tribes. What does he know of God's chosen people?"

Ben heard a noise and looked up. Joel and Micah were coming, carrying their own spotless white lamb. *There will be a lot of sad children on the day these lambs are killed*, thought Ben. But then he remembered why the lambs were to be killed. There would be much sadness on that day for other reasons, too.

Ben thought about that sadness all week. And he was still thinking about it when, on an errand for his mistress one afternoon, he passed a strong-looking, richly dressed Egyptian man on the street. He was laughing and playing with his son, who was only a couple of years old. He would swing the boy up onto his shoulder and then tumble him down as the boy shrieked with laughter. The boy's long hair, bound in back with a cord of red and gold, swung as his father swept him through the air.

It wasn't until Ben had rounded the corner that he realized where he had seen that young nobleman before. His eyes shot open wide, and he turned immediately and flew back down the street, looking for him and his son. Finally he saw them crossing an open square near Pharaoh's palace, and he ran until he pulled in front of them, held up his hand—and couldn't speak. He was out of breath.

The man stopped, his son perched on his shoulder. "What is it, boy?" he asked.

Panting deeply, Ben held up one hand, to indicate to him that he should wait.

"I'm going to be late, boy. Now if you have something to say to me—"

"You saved my life!" Ben blurted between gasps.

The man looked at him curiously.

"Years ago," Ben said. "I fell into the Nile, and you saved me."

The man looked surprised. "So that was you," he said. "And you remember me? You were not much older than my son." And he looked up at the boy on his shoulder. "Well, you seem to have recovered nicely."

Ben nodded. "I owe you my life."

The man chuckled. "Well, if your God keeps visiting us with these plagues, none of our lives will be worth much."

Ben looked deeply into the man's eyes and said, "There will be one more." And then he told the man what would happen the next day, and what he must do for the sake of his son—and Ben prayed that the man would listen and believe.

———

And then the day came. Once again, Ben found himself sitting in the sand behind their home, petting the young lamb and listening as his parents and grandparents discussed what to do.

"None of this sounds like the traditions of our forefathers," Ben's father objected. "Blood on the doorposts, eating the feast with our sandals on—I can't believe that Moses has heard this from God!"

Ben heard his grandfather breathe deeply. "And yet this *is* the tradition of our forefathers, my son. God has, throughout history, raised up men to lead us—some like Abraham, strong and wise and true, and some like Jacob, crafty and weak. And we, God's people, followed them, even the weak leaders. Why? Because it was God we followed, the Master of All. We obeyed God. And if God is calling us to begin a new tradition tonight, with this blood and this feast, then that is what we will do, Moses or no Moses."

"We will perhaps be among the few who actually obey," Ben's father said. "I have heard many of the men at the brickyard scoffing at these new instructions from Moses, and saying that they will not—"

Ben could just imagine Grandfather's response, raising one hand as if to hold off Ben's father's words, shaking his head. "I know, I know. And no one has had more to say against Moses than I have. But—" He paused. "We will obey God. It is He who has turned the water to blood and loosed the hail and the darkness and the locusts on this land, not Moses. And it is He alone who has the power to save us."

And when Grandfather had spoken, there was no more to be said. Ben heard the rattle of metal as his grandfather chose the knife. Then his father appeared beside Ben, holding out his arms for the lamb. Grandfather, holding the thin, sharp knife, stood behind him. Both men were grim-faced. Ben offered the lamb up to his father. And Ben turned his head away as the lamb began to bleat in fear. And when the bleating suddenly stopped, Ben held his face against the warm mud brick of their home and cried.

———

Later, Ben's grandfather dipped a bunch of hyssop into the lamb's blood and slapped it against the doorposts of their home. Then Ben's mother and grandmother roasted the lamb's meat over an open fire and they ate it, all of it. They ate it standing, wearing their sandals and with Ben's father and grandfather eating with one hand and holding their staffs with the other. It had been a strange feast. When Ben asked why, his father had simply said, "Because this is how God said it is to be done. It is the Lord's Passover."

Afterwards, though, his mother had knelt beside him where he sat on his mat and said, "God is telling us that we are, finally, going to be leaving Egypt. And that when we do, we are to move in haste. That is why we stood and wore our sandals as we ate, and why Father and Grandfather held their staffs in their hands, with their cloaks tucked into their belts, as if they were getting ready for a long journey."

There was a sound of laughing, and of people moving past outside, and Ben and his mother both crossed to the doorway and knelt there, peering out around the edges of the doorframe. Drunken men were dancing past, waving their own bunches of green, unbloodied hyssop over their heads, pointing and laughing at each doorway that had blood spread on it. When they passed Ben's house, one of the men saw him peering out. With his eyes wide and a horrible grin gleaming through his dark beard, the man reached grasping fingers toward Ben and growled, "I am the Angel of Death! And I am coming for yoooouuu!" He stepped toward the door, and Ben shrank back into the room behind his mother. He could hear the laughter of the men as they continued down the street.

"I wonder if their wives think this is so funny," Ben's mother said quietly.

"Let us hope they have no sons," Ben's grand- mother said.

For this was to be the final plague: Tonight, the Angel of the Lord would sweep over Egypt, and in those homes where the blood of the lamb had not been shed and splashed against the doorposts, the firstborn son would die. Throughout the land of Egypt.

Even, Ben thought, his heart aching, in the Red House.

He stood. "I want to go see Joel, to make sure that his family has the blood splattered on the door- posts of their—"

"No!" his father shouted, moving toward him and holding out a hand. "You may not leave. None of us may leave this house until morning."

"But why?" Ben asked in a small voice. "I'm worried about—"

"Joel's father will do what needs to be done," Ben's grandfather said quietly. "Tonight, great harm will be done in Egypt. And our only protection against that harm is to do exactly what God says must be done. To the letter. Every jot and tittle. And so we will. He said none of us should leave this home until morning. We will stay here."

———————

Ben lay on his mat that night, in the darkness and the quiet, waiting. He could tell that his parents were both awake as well, and he was sure that, in the next room, his grandparents were also awake. All were waiting.

Before they had gone to their own mats, both of his parents, and his grandparents as well, had come to Ben to say goodnight, to touch his face, to close their eyes and mouth a silent prayer. And as he watched his mother's lips move silently, as he looked at the lines of worry on her face, it suddenly occurred to Ben that this was all for him. The lamb, the feast, the blood on the doorpost—all for him. Both his father and his grandfather had older brothers, still alive and living elsewhere—neither was a firstborn son. When the Angel of the Lord came this night, it was coming only for firstborn sons. And Ben was the only firstborn son in this home. All of this had been for him—all of the effort, all of the worry. The death of the lamb.

The night was surprisingly silent. And very dark.

Ben huddled under his cloak, trembling. Had they made any mistakes? Forgotten anything that God had told them to do? Would he die because they'd done something wrong? Would the angel see the blood on their doorposts in this darkness?

From far down the street, a hideous wailing began, and Ben's heart hammered in his chest. Was that the sound of the angel? No, that was a woman screaming out her grief—and suddenly Ben knew why. Her son had just died. Her firstborn son. Just like him. Ben had to bite his lip to keep from yelling out in fear. It had begun.

Ben heard a quiet, whispering sound, and realized that it was his mother, weeping quietly. She too was frightened. He felt a movement on his mat, and reached out his hand and found hers. She had reached across to comfort him. Or perhaps to reassure herself that he was still alive. They grasped each other's hands tightly. Ben could hear his parents whispering, but could not hear what they said.

Another wailing cry went up, closer now, only a house or two down the street from them, and Ben's mother clutched Ben's hand so tightly it hurt. This time it was the voices of a woman and a man, the parents, no doubt, of a young firstborn son whose life had just been taken by the angel.

The angel was getting closer! Their house would be next!

Ben's heart pounded so loudly it felt as if it would burst out of his chest. And despite the wailing, he felt as if the night was perfectly still, perfectly quiet, waiting, waiting . . .

Lord, You protected me during the darkness, You brought me out of it to my home. Did You save me then only to let me die now? Please, Lord God, my father and grandfather have tried to obey You. Let me live now, to go with them out of Egypt to . . . to wherever You're going to take us. Save my parents from the grief of—

And then a loud scream sounded in Ben's ears, so hideous that he cried out, because he feared that what he heard was the Angel of the Lord standing in the room with him, ready to steal his breath, to take away—

But no, that was no angel—that was a human scream. And it was coming from a house on the *other* side of their house. The *other* side. The Angel of the Lord had passed by. He had seen the blood on the doorpost and had passed by. He was not going to take Ben. His father and grandfather had done everything right. "Every jot and tittle," as his grandfather had said.

Ben's heart still pounded, he still trembled, and

tears stung his eyes. He heard his mother's weeping increase in her relief, and he could tell by the muffled sound of it that she had buried her face in her husband's shoulder as she wept. Ben had to smile, despite his fear and confusion, when he heard, coming from the other room, the almost identical faint sound of his grandmother weeping with her face buried in the shoulder of Ben's grandfather.

And still his mother clutched his hand, stroking his fingers tenderly with her thumb.

She would not let go all night.

CHAPTER 12

Ben visited the Red House one last time the next morning. By the time he returned to his house—the house he and his family were just about to leave forever—his parents and grandparents had packed up all of their belongings. They had even wrapped up the bread dough his mother and grandmother had mixed that morning but had no time to bake. They would have to bake it later. Ben remembered the feast of the night before—eating with their sandals on. It had been true, just as God had said. They would leave in haste.

Runners had come through the village at the first light of dawn, spreading the news: Pharaoh had summoned Moses and Aaron in the middle of the night to tell them that all of the Israelites were to leave Egypt. Today. Now.

And, despite all of the doubt and grumbling and disappointments that they all had experienced in previous months, no one doubted that, this time, following that horrible night that none would forget, this was the day on which all of them would leave. To where, they did not know. But today, Moses would lead the Israelites out of Egypt.

Even his lordship at the Red House had agreed that it was best. Ben had stood with him in the room where the small, cloth-wrapped body of his young son lay, candles and incense burning around it, while they waited for the wagon to come take the body to be embalmed. In a voice hoarse with grief, his lordship had said, "Pharaoh should have agreed to Moses' demands months ago." He had gestured toward the white form of his son. "No offense, Ben, but if your people don't leave now, there will soon be no one left alive in Egypt."

With tears in his eyes, Ben thought about that spoiled, affectionate and gentle young boy who had run through the house with such energy. Now still.

Then her ladyship had given Ben a small packet of gifts to remember them by. When, later, Ben had looked inside, he had gasped in surprise. There was gold! Enough to help his family begin a new life in whatever place God led them to.

His father and grandfather had found some boards from somewhere and enlarged his grandmother's little cart. It was still small, but their possessions were so few that it held them all.

And as they pulled it through the streets to the

fields north of the village where the elders had in-
structed them to gather, Ben saw death even in the
streets of their all-Hebrew village. In the doorway of
one house—a house with no blood on the doorposts—sprawled the body of a man. His eyes were
open but dead, and his mouth hung open, lips slack,
through his black beard. With a shock, Ben realized
that this was the man who had danced mockingly
through the streets the night before, teasing Ben that
he was the Angel of Death, come to take him.

And Ben felt a shiver of fear, much as he had felt
during the night, fearing for his life. Woe to him
who mocked God!

———

All that day, the Israelites came from Goshen
and all over Egypt to gather in the wide fields near
Ben's little village. The women built fires and baked
the dough they had brought with them. And all day,
Ben and Joel and Micah—under strict orders from
their parents not to stray out of sight—had watched
the size of the crowd grow to fill the fields. Ben was
amazed. He had had no idea that there were this
many Israelites. There must have been more Israelites than Egyptians! No wonder the Egyptians were
afraid of them!

And Ben was amazed too at the number of animals. Ben's family owned no animals. But some of the groups that came to the fields that day brought with them *herds* of animals, even cattle. Ben wondered how Moses would find food for all of these people and all of these animals, because most of the people he saw, like his own family, had brought little with them, and probably had food only for a few days, if that.

And then word came, called back and forth through the vast crowd: Moses had said it was time to begin. Belongings were quickly repacked, fires stomped out, babies picked up. And slowly, that immense body of people began to move. Ben and Joel and Micah kept together, almost trembling with excitement, avoiding the still-glowing embers of fires. Surrounded by the shouts of mothers to their children and the bawling of cattle and sheep, Ben and his friends and his family walked away from Goshen, away from the only home Ben had ever known, and toward—well, Ben had no idea what they were heading toward.

"Where are we?" he asked his father one evening a few days later, when they stopped for the night.

His father pointed down a gentle, sandy slope toward a wide, still sea. "That's the Red Sea," he said. Then he looked back the other way. "I'm told Migdol is back there. I've never been this far from Rameses before."

"Are we still in Egypt?"

Ben's father shrugged. "I think so."

At least there was no reason to worry that they were lost. God had performed another wonder for His people. He had sent an immense pillar of cloud that moved ahead of them; all they had to do was follow it. Ben glanced up at the cloud now as it reddened and brightened with the sunset, and felt reassured.

As they sat down to their food that night, word began to spread quickly and quietly among the many thousands of people camped there. It was just a rumor at first, quickly dismissed by most. But soon the voices grew louder:

"Pharaoh is coming after us!"

"Look! I see the dust from his army and his chariots!"

And when Ben and the others stood to look, it was true: There on the horizon, back toward Migdol, was a smudge of dust. Someone was pursuing them.

The Israelites left their dinners unfinished and crowded toward Moses. "Why did you bring us here to die?" some shouted. "We could have died back at our homes, or stayed slaves—which at least would be better than dying in some forsaken corner of the desert none of us have ever seen before!"

Moses raised his staff for silence, and eventually the people quieted down.

"Do not be afraid!" Moses shouted. "Stand firm and you will see the deliverance the Lord will bring you today. The Egyptians you see today you will never see again. The Lord will fight for you; you need only to be still."

And then Moses gazed up into the sky, seemingly in prayer. And while he prayed, the pillar of cloud began to move. Ben watched, amazed, as it moved slowly from in front of the Israelites, around the side of them, and finally positioned itself right behind them, between them and the army of Pharaoh. They could no longer see Pharaoh's army—nor, Ben realized, could the soldiers see them.

Uneasily, the Israelites finished their meals and unrolled their mats on the sand. As Ben lay under the stars that night, trying to sleep, looking up at the thousands of bright stars in the clear desert sky, the wind picked up from the east. Stronger and stronger it blew, all night long. It was a warm wind, a desert wind. And Ben sensed something in that wind—he didn't know what, but it was something God was doing to protect His people. Yes, God is someone to be feared. But He is also someone to be trusted.

CHAPTER 13

Ben had thought that he would get no sleep that night, but before he knew it, Joel was shaking him awake. "Come quickly!" he said. "You've got to come see what Moses has done!"

The warm desert wind was still blowing strongly as Ben shook his head to clear the fog of sleep, rubbed his eyes, and struggled to his feet. Then Joel was off, running as fast as he could toward the Red Sea, and Ben tried unsuccessfully to keep up. It was still the time of first light, gray and dim. The sun would not come up for a long time yet.

Even though there was little light, before they reached the water's edge Ben stopped dead in his tracks, still surrounded by sleeping Israelites.

Before him, right across the middle of the wide sea, there stretched a path of dry sand. On either side of the dry path, the water of the sea was piled into high walls—with nothing to hold it back! The walls were high and steep. Ben thought that,

churning inside them, he could make out the shapes
of fish and other water creatures.

Joel laughed and danced at the edge of the sea.
"Look!" he cried. "God has given us a path to escape from Pharaoh!"

Ben shook his head dully. He didn't see escape in
that path across the sea. All he could see was himself
getting out into the middle of the sea and then the
water walls collapsing and all of the water of the sea
rushing back in over his head, and he would find
himself once again deep under the water, looking up
at the surface that he would never reach.

And what was to stop crocodiles and hippos
from coming out of those water walls and attacking
the Israelites as they crossed?

Around him, families were awakening and getting slowly to their feet, discovering the wonder that
had happened during the night.

"Boys." It was Ben's father. He put a hand on
Ben's shoulder, another on Joel's. But he was not
looking at them; he was looking at the path across
the sea, and his voice was quiet with wonder. "Come
back. Have something to eat. We must get ready to
leave."

All of them turned reluctantly and struggled
through the growing crowd back to their campsite.
Ben's mother handed out to them a simple breakfast:

bread and cheese and water. "Hurry and eat," she said. "I'm sure it's almost time to leave."

The boys gobbled their food, and then Ben's mother shooed Joel back to his own campsite. "Help now, Ben. We must get everything packed away and back into the cart." She began rolling up the mats the boys had been sitting on.

"Are we going to go . . . you know . . . across that path?" Ben asked fearfully.

His mother put her hands on his shoulders and looked into his eyes. "Yes, I'm sure we are, Ben. Who do you think opened that path through the water?"

"God did."

She nodded. "Yes. And if God has opened that path and told us to cross it, then we must obey Him. And we can trust Him not to harm us. We are His people. Would you rather face Pharaoh's army?"

That was a harder question than she knew. Ben wasn't sure which frightened him the most.

But she didn't wait for his answer. "Hurry now. Pack and load." She turned away.

And Ben did manage to help pack, but he wasn't sure how. His mind was churning, and his hands were trembling. How could he step onto that path across the bottom of the sea, with those walls of water towering on either side?

In a few moments, Ben's father jogged up from wherever he'd been. "Moses is telling us all to cross now," he panted. "Is everything ready?"

"Yes, son," Ben's grandmother chuckled. "While you've been off investigating these wonders, we've been working."

"Good," he nodded. "Let's begin." He lifted the front of the cart and began to pull.

Just then Ben heard a voice calling: "Ben!"

He looked around and saw Joel waving him over. "May I walk with Joel?" Ben asked.

Ben's mother looked across the crowd until she saw Joel's family and waved at Joel's mother. "All right," she said. "But stay right with Joel's family. Don't wander off, you and Joel." And then she turned and followed the rest of the family as they headed down the slope toward the sea.

Ben watched them go until other Israelite families, with their flocks of sheep and goats and cattle, got in the way and he couldn't see them anymore. When he turned back toward Joel's family, all he could see were several large cows, moving slowly. A couple of loud-mouthed girls were trying to drive them toward the sea and not having much luck. Ben tried to get behind them so that he could cross toward Joel's family, but after the cows came a long line of people pulling heavy carts, surrounded by families yelling to each other, and by the time Ben found a break in that line and rushed through to find Joel, he realized that he'd gotten turned around, and he had absolutely no idea where Joel and his family were. He was lost in a vast, noisy, crushing crowd of people and animals and carts and wagons.

The first rush of terror when he realized he was lost didn't last long. And Ben knew why. If he'd found Joel and his family, he would have had to follow them down onto the path across the sea. Was he more afraid, as his mother had asked, of Pharaoh's army or of crossing the sea? He didn't know.

Maybe he wouldn't cross the sea at all.

But why are you still frightened? Ben asked himself. *Don't you remember that you promised yourself to get rid of these fears, to stop acting like a baby? There are little children already crossing on the path God has made—babies, and they're not afraid.*

But they had never almost drowned. They had never sunk to the bottom, looking up at the surface they could never reach. Ben was afraid, and that's all there was to it.

He thought of Enoch. Enoch was brave and wise. What would Enoch do?

He would pray.

All right, then, Ben would pray too.

And Ben pushed through the crowd until he came to a small group of trees that formed, between their trunks, a small space. And he crawled into that small space and lay down on his face, while all around him thousands of people and thousands of animals crowded noisily toward the Red Sea.

And as he prayed, Ben remembered, one by one, the plagues God had sent to persuade Pharaoh to let the Israelites go.

Turning the water into blood.

The frogs.

The gnats.

The flies.

The death of the livestock.

The boils.

The hail.

The locusts.

The darkness.

And the last plague: the death of the firstborn sons.

And yet, through all of those things, Ben thought, *God somehow kept His people safe—and even those Egyptians who obeyed Him were saved from some of the plagues.*

So couldn't that same God be trusted to protect Ben now?

What about when I fell into the Nile? Why

wasn't God protecting me then?

There was no use in denying it: Ben was terrified, still, of water, and did not want to go between those walls of water on that path, no matter who had created it, or why.

Ben scrambled up into one of the trees so that he could see, straining his eyes in the still-dim light. On the seashore below him, the Israelites and their animals were stepping onto the path through the sea. Some moved slowly, fearfully, glancing at the walls of water. Some looked behind them toward Pharaoh's still-hidden army and ran quickly onto the path.

Ben watched carefully. Nothing reached out from the walls of water and pulled the people in. There were no crocodiles, no hippos, no hidden pools to fall into—in fact, as near as Ben could tell from this distance, no one was even getting wet. And yet Ben was—

"Papa!" cried a tearful voice. "Papa!"

Ben looked down. Near the trunk of the tree cowered a small boy, only a couple of years old. Tears streaked his face, and his nose was running. He was dressed in rich clothes. And he was not an Israelite—he was Egyptian. And his long hair was bound in back with a cord of red and gold.

The last time Ben had seen this boy, he had been

sitting on his father's shoulders while Ben talked to his father, in the city of Rameses.

This was the son of the man who had saved Ben's life.

And he was alive! Which meant that his father had listened to Ben, and slapped lamb's blood on the doorposts of his home.

And he was here . . . but why? And what was going to happen to him now?

Ben crawled quickly down from the tree and knelt in front of the frightened boy, who stopped yelling and popped a thumb into his mouth. Ben wiped the boy's messy face on the hem of his tunic. "Can't find your papa?" Ben asked. The boy shook his head.

"Out of the way!" someone bellowed, and suddenly a herd of goats was all around them. Ben pulled the boy into the shelter of the trees. Then he looked down toward the water, searching for a tall Egyptian man. But in all of those thousands of people . . .

He looked back—only to find that they were now near the end of the crowd of Israelites, and the tall pillar of cloud was growing nearer, undoubtedly with Pharaoh's army right behind it.

The sun would not be up for some time yet—daybreak was just beginning to paint the clouds of the east in pale pink and orange—but the sky was light. Ben looked both directions one more time— ahead toward the path across the sea, back toward Egypt—and made the hardest choice he had ever had to make. Then he knelt in front of the boy again. "Come on," Ben said. "I'll help you find your papa." And he took the boy's hand and stepped out of the trees into the churning, bawling mass of people and animals.

Ben had no time to look for the boy's father as they walked. He was too busy trying to keep himself and the boy from getting trampled by cattle or run over by heavily-laden wagons. And before he knew it, they were at the edge of the Red Sea—although now, at least right here, it was dry.

Ben stopped, and the boy stopped right beside him. But before he could even think about what he was about to do, a fat woman bumped into him from behind. "Oh, sorry, sweetheart," she said. "But move along, please—hurry! There are many of us here waiting to get across!" And she put her heavy hand on Ben's back and pushed him gently but surely ahead. And Ben stumbled forward a few steps—and then there he was, with the walls of water on either side of him. They weren't high here near the edge, where the sea was shallow—only as high as his ankles. He picked the boy up and held him in his arms when a large ram appeared suddenly beside them. Then the fat woman's family crowded in behind, pushing them several steps further ahead. Ben glanced at the walls of water—as high as his waist now. Ben scurried out of the way of a large cart on the other side, and scrambled to get around some rocks in the path. Without looking, Ben could tell that the walls of water were higher than his head. If they collapsed around him now, he would be under water...

Don't look, Ben told himself. *Keep walking. Look straight ahead. Keep your eye on the shore.*

In the distance, Ben could see the thousands of Israelites—with his own family somewhere among them, and Joel's too—who had already crossed and were now milling around on the opposite bank. *You'll be there soon.*

"Now, you see?" he said to the boy in his arms, who was starting to get heavy. "We'll be across in no time and then we'll find your papa. You aren't afraid, are you?"

And the boy looked back into Ben's eyes and shook his head. Then he put his head down on Ben's shoulder.

No, of course he's not afraid, Ben thought. *All he has to do is relax in my arms, because he thinks*

I can do anything. He shifted the boy in his tired arms.

For the next few minutes, Ben had all he could do making sure the two of them didn't get run over by the crowd of people and animals. When he looked up again, he was amazed at how close they were now to the other side! While Ben had been dodging cattle and carts, they had crossed most of the sea! He moved faster, wanting to cover the rest of the distance as quickly as possible. The ground beneath his feet grew steeper as they climbed up from the sea bottom.

"My son! My son!" a voice cried, and the boy in Ben's arms lifted his head quickly. A tall, richly dressed man ran down the path toward them, dodging people and animals. The boy lifted his arms to him and began to wail.

Ben offered the boy up to him as the man reached them, and he clasped the crying boy tightly, his eyes closed in relief. But the crowd behind them didn't allow much time for the reunion. "Move it along now—there are still many behind us!" people shouted. And the man put his hand on Ben's shoulder and guided him quickly up the slope toward the bushes along the shore.

"You have saved my son's life not once now, but twice," the man said. "I listened to what you said, and decided to obey the God of Abraham, Isaac, and Jacob—your God. And God honored my obedience—the firstborn sons of all of my neighbors and friends died in the night. But not my son." And the man buried his face in the neck of his now-quiet child. "I have decided to follow your God wherever He leads me," the man continued. "What choice do I have? He is God. And I will not forget you, my young friend."

"Look! Pharaoh and his army!" someone yelled, and everyone looked back toward the distant opposite shore of the sea. It was true. The pillar of cloud had lifted, and Ben could just make out the horses of Pharaoh's army rushing from side to side, and rows of chariots moving slowly toward the path. Ben could just imagine the surprise of the soldiers, now that they could see the wonder that God had wrought during the night. But that surprise did not last long, and the army began to charge.

It was a magnificent sight, even though these soldiers were the enemies of Ben's people. Their armor and weapons flashed gold in the growing light, and even at this great distance, the tiny horses looked powerful and beautiful.

"Quickly!" People began to call to those still on the path. "Pharaoh is coming! Come quickly!"

And those few stragglers rushed to the shore,

helped by those who had already made it, and in just a few minutes, all of the Israelites were out from between the walls of water.

But what now? Would Moses command them to flee across the hills? Ben looked back to where he stood, high on a rocky place behind them. He stood motionless, looking back across the sea.

And so they stood and watched as an odd thing happened to Pharaoh's army. When they got to the middle of the path, they seemed unable to come any further. Maybe the chariots bogged down in the sand. Or maybe the wheels of the chariots came off. For whatever reason, the army stopped, milling around in the middle of the sea.

And suddenly the sun rose above the ridge of hills to the east, flooding the valley with golden light. The massed Israelites with their animals on the shore of the sea, the sea itself, and the army of Egypt's Pharaoh, circling in confusion in the middle of the wide path God had made—all of them glowed golden.

Ben looked back at Moses, silhouetted against the rising sun. And slowly, Moses raised his staff, pointed out across the sea, until his arm was high above his head.

And Ben looked back toward the water. Pharaoh's army, it appeared, had started to flee back

toward the opposite shore. But it was too late. Starting on the far side, the shore toward which they fled,
the walls of water began to collapse, to topple over,
and the path began to fill with water—slowly at
first, and then faster, and then so quickly that horses,
chariots, and soldiers were swept away by the force
of it, and disappeared under the water.

An entire army was disappearing beneath the
roiling surface of this sea, and neither they nor their
horses would ever make it to shore. People were
dying right before Ben's eyes.

Then, for some reason, Ben tore his eyes away
from that horrible drama and looked closer, where
the walls of water still held, on the near side of the
sea. And a shock of sudden fear washed over him.
Because there, still standing down on the path that
split the sea, out where the walls of water were high,
was one Israelite everyone had forgotten about:
Micah.

Clearly, Micah had somehow gotten separated
from his family as they had crossed the sea and had
been distracted by the shining, shifting wall of water.
He had always been fascinated by anything bright
and shimmery. Now he stood, motionless, only a
hand's breadth from the water, his nose nearly
touching it.

Ben looked frantically around him. Where was

Joel? Where was his family? But he saw only strangers.

Ben pushed through the crowd around him down to the edge of the path. "Micah!" he yelled. "Micah!" But of course Micah paid no attention. Maybe he couldn't even hear above the noise.

Again he looked around. "Joel!" he yelled. "Father! Mother!" No one answered. Wherever his family was, they couldn't hear him.

And then there were familiar faces—he saw the same boys who'd taken such pleasure in teasing him before the plagues began. He ran up to them, but they barely noticed him, still watching the waters closing over the army of Pharaoh. "Look!" he told them. "It's Micah—he's still out there!" And he pointed.

Their eyes reluctantly followed where he pointed, but they didn't seem concerned. "Hey, it's Eggshell. He'd better get out of there," one boy said.

"But you know Micah," Ben protested. "Somebody has to go in there and get him."

They laughed. "Are you kidding? Why should we risk our lives to save a dummy? Forget it, Riverboy."

"Hey," one of them said. "Why don't *you* go get him, Riverboy?" They all laughed. "You like water so much, you won't care if you get a little wet saving a dummy."

Ben turned away and tried to get the attention of some of the adults gathered there near the edge of the sea. But there was so much noise—from the people, from the wind, from the crashing of the water as the walls collapsed. Some of the adults didn't hear him at all; others looked as if they were in a trance.

There was no one to rescue Micah.

No one, that is, except Ben.

The boy who was afraid of everything. Especially water.

Ben stood a moment longer, watching the walls of water collapse over the rest of Pharaoh's army, washing out the dry path the Israelites had just crossed, the crashing together of the waves as the sea returned to its bed, closer to Micah, closer . . .

Thoughts raced through his mind, seeming to take forever: first, the horrible memory of the day he nearly drowned, the water closing over his head, the mocking sun high above, wavering through the water . . .

Then lying on his mat in his home back in Egypt, trembling in fear, as the Angel of the Lord passed over his house, taking firstborn sons before his house, and after his house—but passing over Ben because his father and grandfather had believed God, and had obeyed Him. God had saved him then. Would He let him die now?

And then, with a yell, without realizing how his

feet had begun moving, Ben was racing down the slope onto the path between the walls of water—walls that had now closed as far as the middle of the sea, and were rapidly closing toward Micah, toward Ben, faster and faster . . .

Ben leaped over rocks. "Micah!" he yelled, but still Micah didn't respond. "Help me, God!" Ben yelled, shouting for God's help, screaming to make sure God heard. "Hold back the waters until we are safe, God, please!"

All Ben could see beyond Micah was the crashing together of the walls of water. Whirling in the waves he could see a helmet from one of Pharaoh's soldiers, a spear, the saddle blanket from someone's horse.

And then he was there, and Ben grabbed Micah, who began to wail and fight him off. But Ben wasted no time or effort trying to comfort Micah or ward off his blows. He simply dragged the screaming boy behind him toward shore.

And then Micah tripped and fell, sprawling face-first into the sand, and Ben, holding tight, fell with him. Gritty sand filled his mouth, and his eyes stung as sand flew into them too. Spitting it out of his mouth, he dragged Micah to his feet and pulled him steadily toward the shore. The walls of water were still more than head-high on either side, and another scene flashed through Ben's mind: the way the sun had looked as he sank toward the bottom of the river years before . . .

He looked up to see how far they had still to go. So far! They would never make it. The shore was lined now with people calling out to them to hurry, reaching out to help pull them to shore—but still much too far away.

Micah rained blows on Ben, screaming in anger and fear. But Ben hardly felt them, so intent he was on getting himself and Micah to that line of shouting people who lined the shore.

Ben was vaguely aware that the walls of water seemed lower now, perhaps no higher than his head. And then Micah fell once more, and Ben grabbed him around the waist with both arms and pulled him up.

Even louder than Micah's yells was the crashing of the water, sounding as if it was right at their heels, the sound of the seagulls wheeling overhead, the shouts of the people on the shore . . .

And then he was scrambling up the steeper slope at the shore, arms were reaching out to him, and someone grabbed him powerfully by his upper arms and yanked him the rest of the way. He felt Micah being pulled from his grasp, and suddenly he was in someone's arms, safe on shore—just as the water came together with a crash behind him, and waves from the collision of the walls of water splashed up onto the shore, getting everyone there wet. But now they all laughed.

Yes, even Ben found himself laughing, though he was also trembling so hard he had to concentrate to keep his legs from collapsing under him. He'd just gotten splashed, soaking him from head to foot, but he didn't feel that surge of fear he had always felt when water covered him. Instead, only relief and thankfulness.

He turned and looked back over the water. Clear across the Red Sea from the churning water at their feet to the distant shore, stretched a path of disturbed water, still sloshing back and forth and covered with foam, over which seagulls swooped and called.

And then someone grabbed Ben tightly from behind, and Ben heard his father's voice in his ear: "Benjamin! Oh, Benjamin! We couldn't find you, and then we heard people shouting and we looked back toward the water—"

And then his mother was there as well, and Ben also saw Joel's father scoop up Micah in his arms, and for once Micah didn't resist.

"This one saved the other boy's life," someone said, patting Ben's shoulder. "Ran back out onto the path across the sea just as the water was collapsin'. Nobody else would go, but he did."

Joel's father, his eyes filled with tears, reached across and ruffled Ben's hair and nodded. "We thought we'd lost Micah. He got separated from us somehow in the confusion. Ah, but Ben, my lad, you found him. What can I say? How can I ever thank you?" Ben felt embarrassed, and hid his face in his father's side for a moment.

God didn't take away the danger, Ben thought. *The water still crashed behind me. And I was still afraid. But God helped me to do what I needed to do anyway.*

You did it, didn't You, Master of All? You sent the Egyptian man to save me when I fell into the water and couldn't help myself. Then You showed Pharaoh and the Egyptians that You are mightier than any of their gods—that You are the only God. And then You saved us from Pharaoh's army, and saved Micah and me from the water—You did it all. Master of All, I love You.

Ben heard someone running up and skidding to a stop right beside him. "What happened?" he heard Joel call out.

Joel's father laughed. "Your friend Ben saved Micah's life, that's what happened. He would have drowned."

Ben turned and looked at Joel.

"You . . . you went back into the sea—after Micah?" Joel asked quietly. "But you could have been . . . you had to . . ."

"But I wasn't," Ben said.

"Weren't you afraid?"

Ben nodded.

Joel looked at his friend quietly. "But you went anyway." He grinned. "And look at you! You're soaked!"

The two boys laughed. "I guess I lived through it," Ben said.

Joel looked over Ben's shoulder, then smiled and pointed. Ben looked behind him, and there stood the boys who liked to tease him. But they weren't teasing now—and, Ben suddenly realized, they would not be able to tease him again—not about his fears, anyway. The boys stood quietly, simply watching him. Those faces that so often had looked at him with contempt now wore expressions of respect and interest.

Ben and Joel looked at each other and grinned. Joel leaned toward Ben and whispered in his ear, "If they call you Riverboy now, it'll mean something entirely different—they'll be thinking of the time you risked your own life to save someone else. That's something they'd never have been brave enough to do."

The crowd around them began to murmur, and soon they heard someone say, "Moses is beginning to sing! It's a celebration!"

"What's he singing?" someone else asked.

Ben's father still held Ben under his arm, and together they turned toward the hill behind them, where Moses still stood, high on the rocks above them.

"It's a new song, I think," Ben's father said. "But I can't quite hear the words."

Soon they could hear them, though, as all the people began to catch on, singing with Moses.

I will sing to the LORD,
for he is highly exalted.
The LORD *is my strength and my song . . .*

Ben looked at the joy on the faces of the people around him as they raised their hands toward heaven, faces turned upward.

The LORD *is a warrior;*
Pharaoh's chariots and his army
he has hurled into the sea.
The deep waters have covered them;
they sank to the depths like a stone.

High on the hill, near Moses' rock, Ben saw an older woman, about the age of his grandmother,

begin to dance, swaying back and forth with a tam-
bourine in her hand.

"It's Moses' sister, Miriam," someone said.

By the blast of your nostrils
the waters piled up.
The surging waters stood firm like a wall.

To Ben's surprise, even his mother and grandmother began to dance along with Miriam, as did
all of the other women, clapping their hands, singing, taking small dancing steps. Ben looked up at his
father, and his father looked back down at him,
squeezed his shoulder, and laughed as he sang.

And suddenly, as much as he was enjoying the
song, the dance, the memory of what had just happened, Ben could hardly contain his excitement to
begin this journey—to wherever God would lead
them.

Who among the gods is like you,
O LORD?
Who is like you—
majestic in holiness,
awesome in glory . . .

Letters From Our Readers

Which story is true? This one or *The Prince of Egypt* one?

Faith L., Grand Rapids, MI

Neither is totally true. Each story is based on the Old Testament of the Bible in the book of Exodus, chapters 4–15. Both our story and *The Prince of Egypt* are an attempt to show people what it must have been like to live then and experience those amazing and scary events. *The Prince of Egypt* looks at the events from the eyes of Moses, while *Trouble Times Ten* looks at the events from the eyes of a child.

The most important part of the story is the real part—about God being the One and Only True God. We can trust that God has us in His hands even when everything else seems to point to the contrary.

I never thought about the plagues that much. Were they really that bad?

Signed, Rob Decker, Sellersville, PA

Yes, they were really that bad. We ran out of room in telling this story, so could not fully describe what it must have been like. I think the scenes that tell about the gnats and the locusts were probably the most accurate.

I'm glad I didn't live back then.

Eric A., Atlanta, GA

I'm glad I didn't either. Bees who attack my picnic in the summer are bad enough.

God seems so mean. He hurt everybody.

Devyn S., Lincoln, NE

God had to show all of Egypt and all of Israel that He was all powerful. I think the plagues were as much to show the people of Israel that He was the one calling them out of Egypt, as it was to show the people of Egypt that He was more powerful and could defeat all the gods they worshipped. Moses wasn't the star of this show. It was God. He wanted to make sure Israel knew they had to trust Him completely. There were hard times ahead for the Israelites, and they needed to be sure about God. These plagues taught them that they could trust God.

Throughout the Bible you will find passages in which God seems to be mean. Honestly, no one can always understand God. We must trust that God is ultimately good, even while He is allowing death and destruction. He is holy and uses everything to teach us, to lead us and to build strength of character in us. He is scary, but He can be trusted.

Where was the Red Sea?

Angie I., Canton, OH

There are many opinions about the actual location of the body of water called the "Red Sea" in Exodus. Was it a lake? Was it part of the present day Suez Canal?

No one is really sure. And frankly, it doesn't make much difference. It would be best to not get bogged down in minor details and lose sight of what is really important—God's hand working among the people of Israel.

I heard there wasn't really a miracle parting the Red Sea at all. They just crossed a shallow lake.

John Beeboff, Mobile, Alabama

There have been many suggestions about what happened in Exodus 14. Some believe that it was a natural event every year—the strong winds blew, and the waters would move aside on the lake bed.

Others have suggested, as you did, that the "Red Sea" was actually a very shallow body of water and the people waded across.

Even if it happened either of these ways, it was still a miracle. If the "dry land" appeared in sea every year naturally, it was still a miracle that it happened at the precise moment the Israelites needed to cross the water, and that the wind ceased or shifted direction at the precise moment when Pharaoh's army was in the middle of the sea.

In the second case, it would be a miracle if an entire army drowned in a shallow body of water, but none of the Israelites did. Also, the Bible account is very clear that the people crossed "on dry land." It does not say they waded.